Allie Romano

ABOUT THE AUTHOR

Tony Romano is the author of the novel *When the World Was Young* and coauthor of the text *Expository Composition*. Born in a remote village east of Naples, Italy, he has taught high school English and psychology for more than twenty-five years. His fiction has appeared in the *Chicago Tribune, Sou'wester, Whetstone,* and *VIA: Voices in Italian Americana*. He was awarded the Whetstone Prize, and his work has been supported in part by several grants from the Illinois Arts Council, a state agency.

Romano is also a two-time winner of a PEN Syndicated Fiction Project award. Both winning stories were produced on National Public Radio's *Sound of Writing* series and syndicated to newspapers nationwide.

He gives readings of his work in the Chicago area, where he lives with his wife and three daughters.

IF YOU EAT,
YOU NEVER DIE

ALSO BY TONY ROMANO

When the World Was Young

IF YOU EAT, YOU NEVER DIE

Chicago Tales

TONY ROMANO

HARPER ⬤ PERENNIAL

NEW YORK • LONDON • TORONTO • SYDNEY • NEW DELHI • AUCKLAND

HARPER ● PERENNIAL

Some of these stories have appeared in slightly different form in the following publications: "The Day of Settlement" in the *Chicago Tribune* and on National Public Radio's *Sound of Writing;* "If You Eat, You Never Die" in the *Chicago Tribune* and on National Public Radio's *Sound of Writing;* "Treading Water" in *Whetstone,* receiving the Whetstone Prize and nomination for a Pushcart Prize; "Whistle Opera" in *Whetstone,* receiving nomination for a Pushcart Prize; "The Casket" in *Sou'wester;* "Hungers" in *Voices in Italian Americana;* and "Comic Books" in *Bluff City.* "Confidences" and "When the Rains Come" were the basis of an Illinois Arts Council Grant. A version of this book was selected as a finalist by the Associated Writing Programs in their annual fiction competition.

HarperCollins books may be purchased for educational, business, or sales promotional use. For information please write: Special Markets Department, HarperCollins Publishers, 10 East 53rd Street, New York, NY 10022.

FIRST EDITION

Designed by Jamie Kerner

Library of Congress Cataloging-in-Publication Data is available upon request.

ISBN 978-0-06-085794-3

09 10 11 12 13   OV/RRD   10 9 8 7 6 5 4 3 2 1

To my father and mother,
Carmine and Maria Immacolata,
whose table was always abundant

CONTENTS

Contents

ACKNOWLEDGMENTS

I CAN'T THANK ENOUGH THE MANY FRIENDS who helped shape these stories: Henry Sampson, Gary Anderson, Kevin Brewner, Daniel Ferri, Edie White, and the many talented creative writing students at Northeastern Illinois University. A special thanks to Tom Bracken, a fine and patient teacher who generously and tirelessly shares his ideas on craft and beauty year in and year out. Thanks also to friends who provided needed encouragement: Maria Mungai, Billy Lombardo, Barb Pluta, Alyse Liebovich, and so many others in the William Fremd High School English and Social Studies departments and in the Media Center. Thanks to my girls, Maureen, Lauren, Angela, and Allie, for their love and patience, and to my extended family for their support, Nirvair and Anna, the Konwinskis, the Malones, the Stoltmans, the Kellys, the Gallichios, the Klosowskis, and the Hermsens, a true melting pot. Thanks, in loving memory, to Jim Kirincich, my best acquaintance, as he used to say, who loved these stories. Fred Gardaphe was the first editor to take an interest in my work, and I will always be deeply indebted for that. Thanks to Michael Radulescu at MRA for his kind phone calls and e-mails, to which I always look forward. Finally, thanks to two people who made this book possible, Claire Wachtel at HarperCollins, who guides with a light and caring hand, and the diligent and talented agent Marly Rusoff, who knows how to make a person feel appreciated. Everyone should have a Marly Rusoff in their lives.

IF YOU EAT,
YOU NEVER DIE

America

MICHELINO

I'M NOT SURE HOW MAMA PULLED it off. She arrived in America about six months before Papa and I, pregnant with my little brother, Jimmy. She found a job, an apartment, even an old storefront for what would be Papa's shop. She had CUMMINGS BARBER painted in red block letters on the huge picture window, thinking Cummings was a prosperous name. The shop closed after a year or so—only a trickle of regular customers strolled in—but, and this is what amazes me, the name Cummings stuck. In every sense. We were Americans now. Every document I've ever seen lists Cummings—social security cards, report cards, everything except birth certificates for Mama, Papa , and I, which we can't even find anymore, though I'm nearly certain I've seen them; Mama accuses Papa of leaving them behind in Italia. I imagine her haggling with the tired clerk at the Italian consulate, insisting that he write Cummings, not Comingo. "But the papers?" he probably sighed. "I must have the papers." I picture her laughing. "Paper? You no believe? What I gotta do? Go home eh come back? I take day off today eh come by you. I mail paper. You mark Cummings." She played out the same scene, I'm sure, at the Immigration and Naturalization office, the Social Security office, until she probably started believing herself that she was an American. So before Papa even stepped foot in this country, the Comingo line was dead.

Hungers

GIACOMO

FOOD WAS RELIGION IN OUR HOUSE. In her tortured English, Mama always said, "If you eat, you never die," which to me simply meant that dead people no longer eat, but it seemed to make perfect sense to her. Why did I imagine that I could hide the weight I was cutting for the wrestling team?

The first seven or eight pounds were easy. The weight came off mostly from my stomach and the lower part of my chest where the ribs pushed through, and I was able to hide it with bulky sweaters and baggy sweatshirts. After ten or fifteen pounds, my face became more angular and bony, my eyes two hollow sockets, my lips dry and cracked. Then she knew.

I sat there at the dining room table on a Friday night, 106 pounds, 21 pounds under my normal weight. Mama clomped from the kitchen to the dining room carrying dishes full of food, her flat, heavy footsteps shaking the house. Every time she set something down, she eyed my plate with anger. Papa sat across from me sipping wine. My older brother, Michael, ripped off a piece of bread from the long loaf and stuffed it into his mouth, crumbs dropping onto his lap. He ate as much as he wanted but was bone-thin and pale. Like Papa. Mama and I were the stocky ones.

I had another pound to lose. Between dinner and ten p.m. I would lose about a half pound pacing my room, another pound while I slept. That left me at 104 and a half, which meant I could eat a half pound and still be at weight for my first match tomorrow.

Coach and I had planned out the new season. We compared my height, five foot seven, with my body fat, 11 percent, and decided I could safely get down to 98 by the end of the season, where I would do well. Last year at 119 I had lost too many matches by three and four points. Coach always said that I wasn't hungry enough, that the losses would stick with me. And they did, in a way. All summer I tortured myself thinking about third periods where I would be down two or three points and lie there like a dog, content to let the clock run out, feeling almost pride for wrestling six minutes without getting pinned, Coach hollering at me as I lumbered off the mat. One time I thought he was going to bust a blood vessel in his neck. I stared at it, engorged and pulsating, while he screamed, "When are you going to stop letting those galooks push you around? How long you gonna be a mama's boy?" It was one of his favorite expressions, and it soon became everyone else's on the team.

Mama finally sat down, her table filled with mounds of linguini, steaming red sauce lumped with meatballs, sirloin steaks, homemade bread, marinated red peppers, and a giant bowl of leafy salad. My mouth, as dry and cottony as it was, watered. I could eat a piece of meat and drink a glass of water, I figured; that was all.

I reached for a small piece of steak, quietly, but leaning over the whole table, making sure Mama saw me. She reached over, plopped another piece onto my dish, and moved the bowl of linguini close to me. My family all chewed quietly and waited for my reaction. I didn't say anything, not tonight. I looked across at Papa. I thought he vaguely understood why I couldn't eat, but I knew he wouldn't support me. He knew that siding with me would pit him against Mama. During arguments with her, Papa's eyes would glaze over and focus a little beyond her. For years I had thought that this was noble, that my father was above the pettiness of the argument. But now I saw in his eyes only tiredness. He reminded me of myself during third periods. I worried about him, worried mostly that he thought I didn't love him. Lately, Coach and I had been spending time together, not only after school but on weekends, and I sensed that Papa felt awkward and jealous, that he feared Coach was taking his place. I wanted to console him, tell him that no one could take his place, but I wasn't sure I believed it. We didn't seem to know how to talk to each other.

With Coach it was different—not that we talked to each other more—but he always knew what to say. He owned a liquor store and on weekends I'd help him unload the delivery trucks. One time we had to drive to the south side in a hurry to pick up a few cases of whiskey. We were barreling forty-five down a narrow one-way street, cars parked on either side, inches away. We scraped hard against one of them and I pictured a deep gash in Coach's Cadillac door. I looked at him. He kept driving, as if nothing had happened. Finally, he turned to me and mumbled, "That asshole almost tore off my door."

Once a week, it seemed, he took me into his office and lectured me on how good I could be. He'd point to one of his Olympic posters and ask, "What's the difference between you and this guy?" I'd shrug politely, always a little intimidated by his gruffness. I knew no matter how excited I got in the office, a few days later my excitement would level off. I didn't want to make any promises I couldn't keep. I wasn't hungry enough, I guess, and I didn't know how to change that.

I looked at my plate, knowing Michael wouldn't help either. He was twenty, three years older than me, and always made me feel three years younger. He wasn't in college; he worked part-time selling shoes at the mall, but he had all the answers. Wrestling, to him, meant sweating and losing weight. Why would anyone go through all that? he asked when he learned I had joined the team. He didn't really want to know. It was his way of talking me out of it.

I ate my steak slowly, peeking at Mama to gauge her dissatisfaction. She chewed slowly, looking down, but not at her food. Her wary eyes focused a little beyond her plate. I finished my first big piece but only picked at the second.

"Giacomo!" she snapped.

"I'm eating, Mama. Look." I stuck a small piece in my mouth and chomped on it. I had already eaten my half-pound allowance.

"Leave him be," Papa said softly, his head lowered.

She went on eating.

I moved my salad around, worked to pick the oregano off the lettuce with my fork, just to appear busy.

"Giacomo—"

I didn't answer.

"Giacomo, I no tell again. Eat."

I took a deep breath. "I don't feel good."

Her neck was crimson. "You no feel good because you no eat."

"I ate a whole piece, Mama," I cried.

"He did eat a whole piece," said Michael.

I looked up at him in shock. He kept eating, vinegar and oil dripping down his chin. When he glanced up at me, he broke out in an
awkward half grin, the same grin he'd worn when he showed up at
my first match last year after weeks of nagging me to quit.

Surprised by Michael's defense, she banged her fork down,
grabbed my dish, and slapped a huge meatball on it. "If you no finish—you no leave house tomorrow."

"But he's got a match tomorrow," said Michael.

"This no you busyness—"

Michael looked up and laughed. Papa's laugh, but more confron-
tational. "What are you going to do? Tie him up? Chain him to the
table?"

I didn't laugh. She could do worse. She could come to school and
find Coach in the gym, swear at him in her frenzied whirl, ignoring
the crowd that would gather. Sometimes I imagined her showing up
at a match and pulling Coach onto the mat, where they would scratch
and scrape at each other like two howling street cats.

"No finish, he no go," she announced.

"I have to," I pleaded.

"You no eat, you no go," she said firmly.

"But you don't understand. This is . . . *importante*."

"Ah, *importante,*" she said, nodding, and then in Italian: "What's important is that you eat."

"When you were . . . young . . . a girl—didn't you ever want to do something different? *Differente?*"

"Girl?"

"You. When you were a girl. Didn't you ever—did you have dreams—wishes?"

Michael, who spoke Italian only a little better, translated.

She shook her head in frustration, as if to say, What does that have to do with not eating?

"Eat. Talk after."

I looked at my plate. If I ate—and the food smelled so good my stomach ached—I'd be overweight tomorrow. If I didn't eat, I couldn't go. I looked up at Papa. Our eyes met, and I saw pity there, but I wasn't sure if it was for me or for himself. He looked down. "Giacomo, maybe you're going too far. Why don't you listen to your mother?"

The meat was tasteless as I stuffed it into my mouth, one forkful after another, my stomach growing fuller and fuller, as if the meat was patching holes. "So she made you eat?" Coach would ask. "She tied your hand to a fork and tied you to the chair? Tell me, did you enjoy it? All three pounds of it?" And I would listen and shrug, not even bother to try to explain. What would I say? I enjoyed it, but didn't enjoy it?

I shoveled the food into my mouth faster, hoping it would cause me to enjoy it less, hoping it would make me sick so Mama would regret the force-feeding.

She looked at me, her set mouth melting into a frown, then turned to Michael. "When Giacomo baby," she said to him, choking back sobs, "he most die 'cause he no eat. I give my milk three month, but I no have nough. So I give bottle. Giacomo no take. He cry eh cry."

We'd all heard the story before. But it was only a story. It wouldn't change anything. Once I finished, I marched to my room without a word. I emptied out an old coffee can filled with pennies and spat in it. I could spit out a half pound before going to sleep. It was a start. If I had to, I'd throw up in the morning.

I sat hunkered over the coffee can, resting my head in my hands. I could probably fall asleep in this position, I thought, drool dripping down my chin the whole time.

When Michael came into my room, there was a thin layer of wet film at the bottom of the coffee can, not even an ounce. He pulled something from his pocket, the blue laxative box from the top shelf in the medicine cabinet, and handed it to me.

"Thanks," I said. "For everything."

He sat next to me on the edge of the bed and stared into the can. Neither of us spoke for a while.

"Why do you do this?" he said.

"I have to be at 105 by tomorrow."

"I mean why do you do it? The whole thing?"

No one had asked. It had been a long while since I had asked myself.

"It makes me feel good," I said.

I realized, and so did Michael, I think, how ridiculous this sounded with the coffee can at my feet and the blue box on my bed.

"I mean it feels good to win." I waited, grateful that he didn't remind me of how many matches I had actually won. "When you walk out on the mat," I said, sounding like Coach, "you can't hide behind anyone. You win or lose on your own." The words sounded flat, I knew.

"Is it fun?" he asked.

"What?"

He turned toward me. "Is it fun? The practices? The cutting weight? Everything?"

Is it fun? I thought. No. Of course it wasn't fun. Michael had never joined any teams in high school. When he came to watch my matches, I could see that he envied me a little, that he felt he had missed out—not on joining wrestling, but on being a part of a team.

I looked at him. "It's okay," I said. I turned to the window. "It's okay."

No Balls

COACH

I TELL YOU, I'M GETTING TOO OLD for this coaching shit. Ten, fifteen years ago it was different. We'd drive fifty miles 'cause these pussy area schools weren't giving us any competition, parade through the gym looking for the locker room. The wrestlers taping the mats, they'd look at us out of the corner of their eyes, like a bunch of mule deer in the crosshairs of my Remington. Even the coaches looked like they were shittin' in their pants. Today I'm lucky to get twelve guys make weight to fill a lineup.

My five-pounder shows up today two pounds over—it's the first match of the season. I'm thinking, What the fuck am I doing here? I been working with this kid for two years. I bring him to my liquor store for Chrissake, give him a job. I find out later, before the match, he's sticking his goddamn finger down his throat to lose the weight. For that, I give him credit. Maybe all the stories I told him about my state champions finally sunk into that skull of his—those guys did whatever it took.

I keep thinking, one of these years I'll get seven or eight of those hard-nosed kids, the kind I used to get at Dunbar. I'm dicking myself, I know. But I keep hoping. Sometimes I think, Maybe I shouldn't have taken off those couple of seasons back at Dunbar. What was I gonna do? I had to get the store going. When I'm ready to start coaching again, the athletic director tells me I gotta be an assistant. I'm the one who built the program, I tell him. Remember that, asshole?

So I put in for a transfer to pussy Steinmetz. I had the director baffled. Steinmetz didn't even have a goddamn wrestling mat. The first year I patched together some ratty mats from P.E., grabbed a few kids out of the hallways, and threw some crusty singlets at 'em. We didn't win any trophies, but it was a start, I thought. Some start. Ten years later I'm screaming at a kid for being two pounds over.

Anyway, we lose the match today by six points, the six points my five-pounder forfeited. I take him into the locker room to chew his ass out, and before I can get two words out, he starts crying. What am I supposed to do? I chew his ass out anyway. I figure he's gonna bawl harder. But he stops. It's like the kid thrives on my screaming.

Finally I calm down. How do you scream at a kid who sits there and nods and agrees that he fucked up? Why? I ask. Why did you eat? He looks down at his bag and starts playing with the zipper. So I start to chew his ass out again.

He says his mother made him eat. The kid's afraid of his old lady. I didn't know what else to say. The kid's got no balls. And I don't know what to do about it. I'm baffled. I like him, I really do. But how do you teach a kid to have balls?

If You Eat, You Never Die

LUCIA

THE COACH, HE SIT IN MY kitch. He have big stomach, soft like dough. But he have face like flour. He no eat good. Maybe French fry every day. Americano, they eat like dirty animale.

My son Giacomo, he no sit. He stand by frigidate. Hands in pock. He wear T-shirt. Is too small. I see bones. He look at shoes by door. I always tell no leave shoes by door. Every day three, four pair.

The coach, he say, "Mrs. Cummings, I came over to talk about Jim's weight." He point by Giacomo. "You have to understand—"

I check cream puff in oven. If I keep long, they get hard.

"Mrs. Cummings, we had a wrestling match today—"

The tray make hot eh I drop. *"Disgraziato!"* I yell. *"Stupido."* I put cold water. *"Disgraziato."*

Coach, he stand. He say, "Are you all right?"

Giacomo, he no move. Hands in pock.

"Are you all right?" Coach say.

"Yeh, yeh," I tell.

Coach, he sit.

Giacomo say, "She does that all the time."

I run to washaroom eh put cream. When I come back, cream puff hard. Throw in garbage. Make again.

"Mrs. Cummings, could you sit please? For five minutes? Please."

I sit.

He fold hand on table, like man when he come last year eh sell insurance. "We had a match today," he say.

"Match?"

"A game," Giacomo say. He look by shoes.

"We had a game today," Coach say. "Another team came to our school . . . on a bus." He put up hands. Like he drive automobile.

He think I stupid. I no stupid. Is crazy language.

He talk talk talk.

I understand most everything. I no stupid. When I come to this country, I say, "Lucia learn English. Nobody cheat Lucia." So I go to market eh watch. I listen. I understand—no take long. But I no speak *perfetto*. Giacomo eh my other son, Michael, some a time they come to market. When I talk, they run away togeth eh laugh. They make ashame. So I talk loud.

They no understand. I come to this country to make better for my two son. Eh they laugh. I never tell—ten year before, I go to school for three, four week. But no time. I work every day by factory. Sixteen year I work.

Coach, he no stop. "The other team gets to our school. When we start to weigh in—you know, to see how heavy everyone is, Jim is one pound overweight. He's too heavy. So he can't compete—he can't play. No game today for Jim. He busted his— He worked hard for three weeks, and all for nothing.

"I know," I tell. "Giacomo work eh you no pay nothing."

"What?" Coach say.

Giacomo, he laugh.

"Why you laugh?" I tell.

He look by Coach. "She thinks you mean my work at your liquor store."

"No, no, no. I mean the work Jim does at practice every day." He move chair close to table. He talk soft. Like secret. "But it's the same thing," he say. He bring face close. Is red. He make chin touch almost table. He say, "It's the same thing. When Jim works at my store, he doesn't get paid, but he's learning. One day he'll use what he learns. Maybe start his own business. Wouldn't you like that?"

I no say nothing. I listen.

"When Jim works at practice, he's got to have at least a chance later to use what he learns. He gets that chance during matches, during games. Can you see how it's the same thing?"

"No same thing," I tell. "When Giacomo finish school, he no play game. He work. Make money."

"I understand that. But you see—" He shake head. Look by Giacomo. They smile, like Giacomo eh Michael smile by market.

"You have to give Jim a chance to succeed."

"I give chance to eat."

Giacomo, he say, "This is not about eating, Mama."

Coach, he move in chair, look at table like he lose some a thing. He say, "Right now, Jim looks a little pale. His cheeks are sucked in, I know. Once he gets used to the weight though, he'll feel stronger. It's gonna take some patience."

"I no have patience," I tell.

Big fatso, he come by my kitch eh tell that Giacomo no eat. When Giacomo baby he most die 'cause he no eat. I give my milk three month, but I no have nough. My chest, they get hard. So I give bottle. Giacomo no take. He cry eh cry.

"Look," he say. "I know you're worried about Jim's health. But he's fine. Just ask him." He point by Giacomo. "Ask him how he feels."

I look. Pantaloon they no fit no more, they touch floor. I say, "He no look good."

Coach laugh. He laugh like butcher by market when I tell "Too much money."

He say, "Go ahead and ask him how he feels. Ask him why it's important for him to lose weight."

Giacomo, he no move.

"Ask him."

"Giacomo, you want I make soup?"

Coach, he scream. "For Chrissake, ask him why he wants to lose weight."

He come by my kitch eh scream. He crazy. I no sit. I go make cream puff. I clean tray. I shake eh shake, eh tray make noise like rain. My two hand shake. I tell, "Giacomo no eat 'cause you tell No Eat. He no want lose weight. You want. Before when he no play game, he eat all day. You no tell no more my son no eat."

"There's no need to get ex—"

"No tell no more. If Giacomo no eat, he no play game."

Giacomo hit table. He scream, "You're not even listening."

Coach tell Giacomo be quiet. He look by me. "Mrs. Cummings . . ."

He talk eh talk. He say team need Giacomo. I no listen. I cook.

When he leave—*grazie Dio*—I find rosary. I pray he no come back by my kitch. Ask, he say. Ask. What I gotta ask? Is too late. I wish I no come to this country. I wish I stay by *paese,* by farm. Everybody work togeth. Everybody eat. I no understand America. Is crazy.

Five clock we eat. Little salad. Artichoke. Mostaciolli. Steak. Giacomo he look by food. I pray. He see steak. Six, seven big piece. He take fork—*grazie Dio*—eh push eh push eh find small piece, for bird maybe.

I jump. I put fork in. "Is my piece," I tell. Maybe Giacomo he take big piece. I hope.

Giacomo, he look by Michael. He look by me. He stand eh bring face close. "Sit down, Ma," he tell.

"What?"

"Sit. Down." Giacomo eyes, they no move. He make mouth hard, small. Is no Giacomo. He pull meat with fork.

I pull back. "Giacomo!"

He pull eh pull meat, eh blood come out.

"Giacomo."

He pull. He break eh make two piece. I have half. Giacomo have half. He no say nothing. He eat.

Michael, he smile.

I look by Giacomo. I look by my fork. Small piece. Half. For sparrow. For baby. When Giacomo baby, he most die— "Eat," I whisp. Nobody hear. Eat.

Comic Books

Giacomo

I GUESS THE MAIN REASON I HUNG around with Angelo Predo back when I was eleven was that he was almost two years older than me. It didn't matter that everyone at school held their noses when he walked by, more out of meanness than anything, although he did smell sometimes, or that he dressed for school like some D.P. from Italy, with his oversized dress shoes and baggy dress pants, shiny and thin around the seat, held up by a ratty black belt. He'd had to make an extra hole in the belt and squeeze it around his waist as if drawing tight the stringed-top of an old laundry bag. Instead of holding their noses, sometimes they would roll up their pants and prance around with their feet out, chanting, "Wherever I go, dago." Being the only other Italian on the block, I always felt like they were mocking me, too.

But the ridicule never seemed to bother Angelo. He'd flash a huge smile, his nose scrunched, his eyes two cunning slits, as if he knew something that they didn't, as if to smugly suggest, "Laugh now . . .

but I'll show you." Sometimes, along with the smile, he would gesture with his middle finger or wave a salute under his chin. Then he'd walk away.

I never followed. We seemed to have an understanding that, at school, we were on our own. That way, although neither of us had many other friends, he wouldn't have to play with someone two grades below his, and I wouldn't be included in any ridicule. But I would always catch up with him later—though that would soon end.

It was a Friday morning in late August. I got up early because Angelo and I had planned to collect bottles all day. My mother was in the backyard hanging sheets. I dreaded going out there, but I had to.

"Mama, I'm going by Angelo's house."

"What? I tell before. Angelo no good. Why you go?"

The white sheets flapped softly in the breeze.

"We're going to collect bottles, Mama."

"Collec?"

"Collect bottles—bring them to Buddy's."

"Where you find bottle? In alley? In garbage? You make dirty— like Angelo."

I stared at the sheets, the sun reflecting brightly off them. They smelled fresh with bleach.

My mother seemed to enjoy ridiculing Angelo, too. His father was a bum who drank too much, she always claimed. And his mother was a *puttana*. I never knew exactly what *puttana* meant, but I knew it was unholy and sinful because she always flashed the sign of the cross on her chest whenever she said it. She claimed that when Angelo's father came to Chicago from Italy fifteen years ago, he scrambled to find a wife to gain citizenship and married the first *puttana* on the street he could find.

"I won't get dirty, Mama. And Buddy gives us two cents for each bottle."

She grabbed a clothespin from her mouth and fastened it tightly onto the line. She seemed to be considering all the two cents I'd make.

"Okay, no go far. Eh no forget. Come home—eat."

Before she had a chance to change her mind, I took off. When I got to Angelo's house, he was sitting in his gangway, tugging at the emblem on his torn gym shoes. He stood up when he saw me. He wore an old, ash-colored T-shirt that at one time was white. His face was already smudged, his thin black hair stringy and uncombed.

"Let's go, Jim," he said.

Something was wrong. He always greeted me with "How's it going, my man," and then slapped me five.

He turned and walked toward the alley. I trailed behind. As he passed the back door, he said evenly, without turning or stopping, "I'm going."

His father, a can of Pabst at his feet, sat outside the door, his legs crossed, his head back. He puffed on a cigarette, sucking in deep long breaths, his cheeks tightly drawn, and let out thick clouds over his head. He looked blankly into the distance toward the stacks of the factories and said nothing.

I followed Angelo into the alley, making sure to grab the wooden wagon inside the fence. He kept walking.

I lagged behind a few steps, too scared to ask what was wrong. The last time I had seen him this way was after his father had nearly broken his jaw. According to Angelo, his father had come home drunk at four that morning and started arguing with his mother. When Angelo stepped in to help, his father slapped him across the face with the back of his hand. All Angelo talked about that day was running away. First he was going to hop a train; then he decided to hitch a ride to California; he even talked about stealing a car. It was just talk, but he scared me. There was a hardness in his voice I'd never heard before. The following day though—and this puzzled me for a long time—he was back to normal, joking and cussing, as if nothing had happened.

At the end of the alley, I caught up with him and waited for him to say something.

"I hate him, man," he said.

"Your dad?" I asked weakly.

"My dad . . . what a joke! He's not my dad."

I didn't understand. "What do you mean he's not your dad?"

"Ah, forget it."

He picked up a bottle and flung it down the alley, back toward his house. I watched it fly, end over end, then splatter into a thousand pieces. I wondered if we were still going to collect bottles.

"C'mon, Angelo. What do you mean he's not your dad?"

"Forget it, Jimmy."

I hated when he called me Jimmy.

"You wouldn't understand," he said.

I kicked hard at the gravel. He sounded like my mother.

"How could he not be your dad?" I insisted.

He picked up some rocks and started tossing them. We watched them bounce off the telephone pole.

"My old man came home late last night," he said. "Well, I guess this morning he didn't want to get up to go to work, so my mom starts bitchin'."

It looked like he wanted to cry, but I knew he wouldn't. He kept throwing rocks.

"She says we ain't got no money, that she can't even buy me a T-shirt. My old man says, 'Look, you want clothes for him, get a job. He's your son. I'm not even sure he's my son.' They were in the bedroom, but the door was open. I heard him."

I still didn't quite understand, but I didn't want to look stupid.

"He said that?"

"That bastard. I wish he was dead."

The hardness in his voice was back. But this time I knew it wouldn't last. He just had to get it out of him.

I picked up a handful of rocks and joined him, both of us throwing so hard that we barely hit the pole, but it felt good, even the soreness in the elbow and in the shoulder.

After a while, we found ourselves walking to the schoolyard, like we always did, and started collecting bottles. We'd usually find ten or fifteen bottles there that Willie and Ray and all the older guys would leave after the softball game, and we wanted to get them before anyone else did. I guess it wasn't cool for them to be worried anymore about a two-cent deposit.

I looked in the wagon. "That's thirty-two cents," I said.

Angelo stared blankly at the bottles.

"It's a good start," I said.

He nodded absently.

I had to snap him out of his stupid daze.

I picked up a bottle, checked left and right for witnesses, checked again. "Make that . . . thirty cents," I said. I flung the bottle with all my power against the bottom bricks of the school. My arm was so sore that the bottle barely reached. It bounced off intact and rolled lazily back to us.

We stared at each other in disbelief.

"Make that . . . thirty-two," Angelo said.

We burst out in a sudden fit of laughter. I was glad I could make him stop thinking about his father for a while.

By noon we had collected a dollar and fifty-two cents' worth of bottles—or I collected that much. Angelo wasn't much help. We stopped at Buddy's, like we always did, to cash in what we had. I never actually cashed in the bottles, but traded them for comic books, usually *Superman* and *The Hulk*. I started collecting them when I was eight and had every issue since. I even had some from before that time. My brother, Michael, had given me his collection when he started high school.

Angelo walked straight to the candy counter. I rushed to the comic book stand to look at the new issues that arrived that morning. I pulled out a *Superman,* an *Action,* a *Batman,* and a *Hulk,* and I still had enough for a Pepsi.

I turned around, and Angelo was gone. Buddy's wasn't that big—two aisles of canned goods, another aisle for bread and pastries, a candy counter up front, and freezers all around the sides for pop and milk and ice cream—so I was confused. I didn't even see Buddy.

I walked to the back of the store, beyond the swinging doors, where Buddy bought and sold old lawn mowers and fans and radios and other junk. As I trudged farther back, my head swam from being in a new place, somewhere I wasn't sure I belonged. I was amazed at how dark it was in the back room, despite the bright sunshine outside. I knew Buddy didn't have a dog, but I pictured one leaping from one of the dark corners and gashing my eyes out.

I heard Angelo's voice: "How fast will it go?"

"You can get it up to forty-five with no problem."

"Can I take it out back to get a better look?"

"Sure."

I turned the corner and peered down a narrow aisle formed by high shelves on either side. Buddy was pointing a flashlight beam down at a mini motorbike. Squeezed in next to him, Angelo was on his knees inspecting the bike.

I said, "Say, Ang—"

They both let out a startled shriek.

"Hey, I didn't mean to scare you. Sorry."

"What are you sneaking up on us for?" said Angelo, his face turning darker.

"I just wanted to know where you were."

"Why don't we go out back?" said Buddy.

Even with the dim beam of the flashlight, I could make out the giant tattoo on Buddy's right arm: a purplish gray lizard whose tail curled and wrapped itself around its own head. It gave me an eerie chill. It didn't seem right that someone as old as Buddy should have a tattoo. Not that he was old-old, but his dishwater brown hair was thinning on top, like Angelo's father's, and his soft gut hung over the top of his silver belt buckle, which was tarnished and nicked and big as a deck of cards.

I felt like I was in the way. "I'll meet you out front, Angelo. By the comics."

"Yeah, sure," said Angelo.

I had finished reading the *Superman* and the *Hulk* when Angelo finally walked out with the empty wagon, the loose wooden base bouncing and rattling as he pulled it down the big stoop. We built it at the beginning of the summer out of scrap wood, nailing and gluing it, painting it bright green, but the heavy bottles and the rain over the past few weeks were making it look like scrap again.

"We're going to need a new wagon soon," I said.

"Twenty-five bucks."

"What?"

"He only wants twenty-five bucks for the bike."

"Where are you going to get twenty-five bucks?" Right away I was sorry I didn't say "we."

"I'll get it. Don't worry, I'll get it." He started walking. "Let's go find some bottles."

The most we had ever collected was five dollars and sixty-two cents' worth. But I didn't remind him. I was glad he wanted to look for bottles—for whatever reason.

"What are you going to do with the bike, Ang?"

"Huh?"

He'd heard. He was deciding whether to tell me.

"The bike. What are you going to do with it?"

He stopped and looked at me for a while, his eyes glazing over.

"You want to come with me, Jim?"

"What are you talking about?"

His eyes became more focused. "The bike goes forty-five miles an hour. We could be in Florida in three or four days."

"Florida?" I'd been out of Chicago only once.

"I gotta get away from him. I'm tired of it."

I had a wild urge to run home and wrap myself tightly in the sheets in the backyard and sleep and wake up the next morning to find that everything was back to normal. But, I imagined Angelo sprawled on the highway, flattened by the giant wheels of a heavy truck. I thought about Superman, the Hulk, wondered what they would do—maybe take Angelo's father and tie him to the top of a gleaming skyscraper until he agreed to change. And he would change.

My hands were wet. I laid the comic books in the wagon, afraid I'd ruin them. "Yeah, I'll go," I agreed.

"You mean it?"

"Yeah, I'm ready," I said confidently.

I didn't know what else to say. The iciness in his eyes, the evenness in his voice, told me he would get his bike.

"Let's go," I said. "We're going to need a lot more bottles."

By five o'clock we had the entire wagon filled, along with an old shopping bag. I didn't bother to count, but we had about three dollars and fifty cents' worth. I wondered if Angelo realized.

"Giacomo . . . Giaaa-co-mo."

My mother was calling.

"Giacomo . . ."

"Angelo, I gotta go eat." Hours earlier, we had planned to go to Florida, and now I had to go home to eat because my mother was calling.

"I'll take care of the bottles," said Angelo.

"You'll take 'em to Buddy's?"

"Yeah, I'll take care of it."

When I got home, I sneaked into the backyard, and with the hose, washed off the dried-up bottle syrup from my hands and my face. My mother would holler at me all night if she saw me. The sheets, still hanging, seemed stiff and gray.

As I was about to walk into the house, my mother stepped out and shoved a dollar into my hands.

"Giacomo, hurry—go to store. Buy loaf of bread."

"Okay, Mama."

"Hurry."

"Okay."

"No slice bread. Loaf. No forget. Hurry."

"Okay, Okay."

"Careful when you cross street."

I set down my comic books on the back porch and left. I was tired, and just wanted to sit and read them and forget about everything.

When I got to Buddy's, the front door was locked. Buddy lived alone in the apartment upstairs, so I knocked as hard as I could. No one answered.

I went around back to the alley entrance. The back lot was enclosed by a tall wooden fence. I pulled open the gate halfway and peered in. Inside, it was like another long alley, blackwall tires piled high against the back fence, bicycle frames entangled like weeds on one side, and empty milk crates filled with wires and rusted tools against the other. I stuck my head in farther. Next to three steel-drum trash cans was a box filled with old comic books. I walked in and bent down and started flipping through them. How could anyone throw these out? I thought. This was a gold mine of blue masks and red capes and green and yellow glossy covers and God knows—.

I looked up.

Angelo was in the yard. He was behind a stack of tires outside the back door of the store—on his knees, next to the minibike. I could see only his back. Buddy was in front of him, looking down.

He didn't say a word. I held my breath. They were too close to each other. Buddy's belt buckle was unfastened, hanging. He was too damn close.

I turned and crawled to the gate. Crawled like a baby, one step at a time, my knees scraping against the pea gravel. I had to move slowly. I couldn't let him hear me.

I got outside the fence and collapsed, wiped my hot face with my T-shirt. Still on the ground, I eased the gate shut and heard it click softly into place.

I got up and ran. Ran faster than I had ever run. My feet bounced off the pavement like metal springs. My eyes burned.

I had to tell someone. I didn't know if I should go to Angelo's house or call the police or run home. Someone had to get Angelo out of there. I ran to the schoolyard. I thought maybe one of the older guys would help. But no one was there. I ran to Angelo's house, got as far as the front door, but I couldn't knock. I didn't know what to say. I wanted to go back and rescue Angelo myself. But I was too scared.

I ran home. Michael was in the bathroom. My mother was in the kitchen.

"No bread?"

"No . . ."

"I tole you—hurry. He close, no?"

"Buddy's a bad man, Mama."

"You walk and take time and he close, huh? Go wash."

"But, Mama—"

"Go. Now."

"Mama, Angelo's in trouble."

"Ha! I tole you. No play with Angelo no more. Now, go wash."

I looked at the clock. It was getting late. Angelo could be dead by now, I thought. I rushed to the bathroom to see if Michael would listen to me. But he was on his way out. "I don't have time, you see," he told me. He had this habit of adding *you see* to everything he said, and it suddenly annoyed me.

I went in the bathroom and cried. My friend was in trouble, and I'd crawled away from him. My mother called from the kitchen. I didn't answer. She called again. I knew she'd make me eat. I couldn't leave the house without eating. I looked in the mirror and decided. I would eat—then go back. I had to do something.

I rushed the food down in minutes. When I got back to the store, it was still closed. I walked around back again, and the gate was locked. I was too late.

I ran to the schoolyard. I had to tell someone.

Then I saw him—two blocks away. He was riding the minibike, hooting and hollering, a smile spread across his face.

Angelo wouldn't be collecting bottles anymore, I knew.

I slipped into the alley, my eyes raw and wet. When I got home, I locked myself into my room and pulled out the stacks of comics from the drawers in my nightstand. I thumbed through them, spreading my favorites on the bed one by one so I could see them all, hundreds of them. But I couldn't help thinking how grimy they seemed next to the crisp linen sheets.

I stared at one of the *Superman*s. Fiery bullets ricochetted off Clark Kent's square chest, tearing away a patch of his gray suit, a red *S* bleeding through. His black rimmed glasses hung crookedly at the tip of his nose. Lois Lane stood to the side, her mouth frozen open, her wide blue eyes nearly jumping off the cover. I remembered how eagerly I had read that issue. As it turned out, Lois Lane did see the *S,* but Superman discovered a way to reverse the earth's rotation for a while to erase her memory. Like wiping clean a chalky blackboard. I'd felt important after reading that one, as if I were in on a secret, as if anything were possible. But the cover now seemed smaller somehow, familiar yet strangely new.

I packed the comics back in the box, brought them to our alley, and set them inside the cleanest of the three trash cans, one we hardly used. During the next few days before garbage pickup, barely a minute passed that I didn't think about saving those comics, shoving them deep in the closet. But I couldn't stop feeling that they no longer belonged to me, that they weren't mine, really, to reclaim.

One Up

MICHELINO

When I was seven I saw my father shoplift. He pocketed one of those shiny red pencil sharpeners, the size of a yo-yo, with a clear bubble of plastic on top where you could watch the pencil shavings curl up on themselves. It couldn't have cost more than fifteen cents back then. We didn't have a lot of money, but I think even I had fifteen cents. As we marched out of the department store, our gray winter coats bundling us, my father put his arm around me, handed me the sharpener, and flashed this confidential, cunning smile.

"For you, Michelino," he said. That was all he said.

We walked for a while like that, his one hand cuffing my neck, the other holding this hot item in front of me.

I looked up at him, the sharpener still visible out of the corner of my eye, like I could see him and the sharpener at the same time. He seemed to sense my reluctance and nodded reassuringly, did his best to look earnest. This will be our secret, his eyes said. But I sensed he was trying too hard to seem casual, as if he were pleading with me to take the damn thing already. I took it, of course. Stuck it in my pocket the instant my hand touched it. I might have even looked back toward the store to see if anyone was trailing us. It was exciting, I admit that, but I also felt lousy. I mean, this was my father.

It wasn't until years later, as an adult, that I understood any of this. My dad wasn't a thief, you see. In fact, I never saw him lift again. Maybe he was so remorseful—not that he'd taken the thing, but that he'd allowed me to witness and participate—that he reformed. But no, like I said, he wasn't a thief. It was just his way, I think, of showing me that he had one up on someone, that he wasn't going to let Goldblatt's Department Store push him around.

Whistle Opera

LUCIA

MY HUSBAND, HE LEAVE TUESDAY.

He scream. "You are never satisfied," he say. He bark like dog by back alley. He say, "You want to come to America, you want to go back. Italia, Italia. Keep complain and I will go back. I will go back."

I no complain. I joost tell, maybe we have more money if we no come to America. Maybe he buy shop for haircut. Eh no work for Bruno for two, three penny. No complain.

Before, long time ago, eighteen, nineteen year, by *paese*, by farm, Fabio make haircut in base-e-ment. By my house. Is nice, but no too much busyness. So I tell my friend eh they come. Fabio complain. Man only, he say—is no beauty shop. Is busyness, I tell. If dog come, eh he have money in mouth, you give haircut, no?

So Tuesday he leave. What I gotta tell? No go? He come back. I no worry. Nine, ten clock, *O Dio,* he no come. 'Leven. Still he no come. Now I crazy. I take walk eh look. I go by school, by park, up eh down. I see blue light by Bruno shop. I look. He sit by back eh watch TV. I walk eh walk, my stomach make sick, eh he watch TV.

What I gotta do? I go home. *Disgraziato.* I work 'leven year by factory, night, so I no leave Michael eh Giacomo by babysit. I make plastic, piece work, sweat, how much I sweat, support everyone—for what? Nobody care. So I change. I work day.

Wenissday morn, Michael eh Giacomo they eat cereal. Michael he ask where Papa go.

I laugh.

"Why you crying, Mama?"

"What?" I tell.

He look by cereal. Next birthday Michael make fourteen. No fifateen. Fourteen or fifateen. He say, "I said why—"

"Is onions," I tell.

He look eh look. No see nothing.

I go to frigidate eh take onion eh peel. I do fast. Pretty soon Michael cry.

"See," I tell. "Onion."

Michael he wipe eye eh shake head. Giacomo eat.

I wipe hand. I give two dollar for Michael eh two dollar for Giacomo. "Today when you finish school. You no come home," I tell. "You go by shop. Make haircut," I tell.

They look like I crazy, like I need maybe *dottore.* They never make haircut by shop. Always home. Eh they no give money.

Michael say, "But, Mama—"

"Go to school," I tell. "No be late."

"But—"

"Go . . . Now."

They run. I put onion in frigidate eh go to work. Maybe tonight Fabio no watch TV by Bruno shop. Maybe tonight he sleep home.

Four clock I come home eh make pasta e fagioli. Fabio he like so much. Maybe he smell fagioli by Bruno eh—ha!—run home. Tonight I no complain. What I gotta complain? I come to this country eh find job in two day.

I wait eh wait. I hear outside. Michael eh Giacomo they laugh eh run. Fabio he whistle opera. How many time I tell, no whistle, no look like buffoon Italiano. In America—

Tonight I no complain. No tonight.

They come by door eh knock. Three buffoon now, no joost one. I no listen. I make salad. They knock eh knock. I go by door eh open. "Three crazy," I tell. "Why you knock?"

They say, "May we come in?" They say togeth. Michael eh Giacomo smile. Fabio, I don't know.

I put hand by haircut. Is short. *"Speciale,"* I tell. I talk like Americano: "You may comb in," I tell.

They move.

"Wait," I tell. I put hand out, like I collec money in street. "Change?" I tell.

They no understand.

"This morn I give two dollar," I tell. "No cost two dollar for haircut."

Fabio he take four dollar from pock eh give to me, like he pay taxi. He no look good. Maybe he no sleep. Maybe he smoke cigaret all night. Poor Fabio.

"Michael. Giacomo. Go wash," I tell. "Do fast."

They go.

Fabio he no move. I take hand eh pull inside.

"This morn you take bath?" I tell.

He pull hand back eh put in pock.

I joost ask. How you do busyness if you no take bath? Americano they no like a smell. Okay, I no ask, I no say nothing.

He go by washaroom eh close door. Whistle opera. How many time— He stop! Maybe he rememb what I tell. I tell all the time.

We sit eh eat. Michael eh Giacomo they talk base a ball.

"Busyness okay?" I tell.

"You know, Wednesday," Fabio say. "The rest of the week will be better."

Michael eh Giacomo stop talk. Is quiet.

"Factory is okay?" Fabio say.

He no mad. Fabio no stay mad long. I know. He eat eh eat. Three bowl.

We finish eat, eh my boy they help. Bring dish to sink.

Fabio he sit.

"You break leg?" I tell. I laugh so he no make mad.

Michael say, "This is America, Pop. Where do you think you are?"

He throw towel by Fabio face. Towel cover everything, eye,

mouth. Fabio no move. Ten sec. Twenty sec. Then he laugh eh throw towel by Michael. He bring dish by sink.

I wash dish. Rinse. Wash eh rinse. I go fast.

Michael eh Giacomo finish bring dish, eh Fabio dry. Is small kitch. Too small.

"Stop!" I tell. "Out," I tell. "Is too small in kitch. Out. How many time I tell, No . . . Stay . . . in . . . kitch."

Is quiet. I hear frigidate. I hear clock. My hand shake. Fabio, I tell in my head. Fabio. Is Okay. I no mean. Stay.

He look by towel.

"Yeah, Pop," Michael say. "How many times do I have to tell you?"

"Yeah," Giacomo say.

They good boy. They laugh.

Fabio he look by window eh smile eh make noise like laugh too.

I take Fabio by hand eh put hand in soap water. "You stay," I tell. I move close. "I no complain," I whisp.

I leave kitch. Go outside. Pick tomato. Pretty soon I hear Fabio. By window he look outside eh whistle opera.

Milkboy

TONGUE CURLED OUT, JIMMY CUMMINGS STEPS into the batter's box. He clenches his new Louisville and glares at the pitcher, who jumps sideways off the red brick that is the mound and fakes to the plate. The pitcher winds again, bends, and the ball sails out of his hand in a high arc, floats higher, and spins, turns, and sinks near the plate. Jimmy leans forward and swings. He swings with the power of a twelve-year-old who hasn't played softball all winter, who hasn't ever hit a sixteen-inch clincher past the infield. The ball dribbles back to the pitcher. Jimmy lays his unchipped bat down on the asphalt and races down the spray-painted, silver baseline to first. His small legs pump furiously, every sinew and tendon taut with acceleration. He leaps high for the base, stretches. With his foot about to touch down, he hears the ball thud into the first baseman's hands, the third out of the inning.

He overhears them. "Shit, man. Next game you guys get Cummings."

"Right, jack. Anything you say, jack."

Stone-faced, Jimmy walks back to the plate to catch. This is the third time he has grounded out. He doesn't understand. He is stronger this year. He has worked for Mr. Liptak six months now, every Saturday since January, carrying heavy milk cartons up three and four flights of stairs. He can do it without stopping. He should be able to knock a little ball to the chain-link fence. Almost every night he dreams about it—not a homerun, just rattling the fence with a long line drive for a double or triple.

He picks up his thirty-two-inch Louisville by the heavy end and stands behind the plate, tapping the perfect knob of the bat on the greasy blacktop. If he had flung the bat, he thinks, he would have made it. But it is a new bat, his first. He looks at the setting sun, burnt orange and big as a house, knowing that he won't get another turn at bat. He taps harder, finally chips it, and tosses it next to the other bats. Tomorrow is Saturday. After work there will be another game.

The game ends quickly because of darkness, and everyone retreats, like they always do, to the school steps. The three-story school, set where right field should be, is a crumbling fortress. The ornate swirlings at the top are still intact, but the bottom bricks are chipped and crumbling from years of rock-throwing. Large boxes for fast-pitching strike zones are spray-painted onto the white granite slabs. Several windows are broken—the ones that aren't have been replaced with Plexiglas. The concrete steps, wide and formidable, give the school a squat symmetry. Directly above the steps is emblazoned *St. Columbkille*, as if the steps themselves are the school: you can learn how to make your own M-80 firecracker there in the early morning or learn how to play nickel-and-dime poker in the late afternoon; at night you can hide in the darkness at the very top and taste your first kiss. Jimmy can only imagine.

Tonight the steps will be used as the prison box for ring-a-levio. Frankie and George choose sides. Jimmy is chosen last, by Frankie, so his team gets to hide first. They run down the alley in pairs except for Jimmy, who lags behind and watches. Nino and Fran jump over the rectory wall. Mary and Annie duck into Mrs. Keel's yard. Frankie and Joey cut down another alley. Jimmy wants to stay close to the schoolyard so he hides behind the first few trash cans. From there he can hear who gets caught and how many people are guarding the prison box.

As he settles himself behind the cans, the other team races by. He'll have to wait now. Once three or four of his teammates are captured, he'll run out in a blaze past the guards, tag and free his team, and together they'll run down the alley laughing. "Way to break us out, man," they'll say. Then Jimmy will slap everyone's hand and say, "Fucking A, man." No one has ever heard him swear before, but it's time, he decides.

It doesn't take them long to catch Mary and Annie. They should know better than to hide in Mrs. Keel's yard. To Jimmy's surprise, Frankie and Joey are brought in soon after.

It's time. He tries to slow his heart and quiet his breathing so he can hear. He needs to know how many guards there are. He listens: one . . . two—

"Gia-co-mo . . . Giaaa-co-mo."

His mother is calling.

He eases out from behind the cans and crawls to the edge of the schoolyard.

"Gia-co-mo." The voice is louder.

He peeks around the corner of the school: three guards.

"Giacomo."

He doesn't have time to wait for the right moment when the guards' heads are turned.

He gets up and dashes toward the side of the steps. When his team sees him, they stealthily lock hands and stretch to form a line from the stairs to where Jimmy is storming. All Jimmy has to do is tag Frankie at the end of the line and they'll all be free. He is twenty feet away, fifteen—

The guard closest to Jimmy suddenly turns, cuts between Jimmy and Frankie, and yells for help. Jimmy has to circle left. He can't get tagged himself. He runs blindly. As he's about to cut back toward the stairs, he looks up and freezes.

His mother is standing in the middle of the alley, slapping her thigh with a flat, black slipper. She moves toward him.

Without thinking, Jimmy starts running, determined to free his friends. The guard who cut him off nearly tags him. The other two guards join the chase, yelling, screaming directions.

His other teammates, Nino and Fran, hear the screams and come out of hiding to help. It's three-on-three now. They all rush the box, retreat, weave in and out between the guards in waves.

Waving her shoe in the air, Jimmy's mother advances, screaming, "Giacomo. Giacomo. *Veni qua,* Giacomo."

Nino gets tagged from behind. Fran falls and is captured easily. It's three-on-one now. Four-on-one with Jimmy's mother.

When the guards realize they have help, one by one they stop running, stop yelling. They sit on the steps, their eyes wide.

Jimmy's mother keeps chasing, reaching out to whack her son across the ear when she can, her other slipper scraping and slapping against the asphalt. "*Veni qua* . . . Ay."

Jimmy is much faster than her. He runs, stops, starts again, finally surrenders, not sure what to do. His mother grabs him with one hand and drags him across the schoolyard.

"Why you no come when I call—eh?"

She lifts his collar.

"Why you no come?"

She keeps repeating the question, whacks him across the back of his pants when he doesn't answer. He tries to deflect the blows with his hand, tries to loosen her grip by buckling his knees, but she pulls harder.

"You wanna job you gotta sleep. No easy. Mr. Lipek he home—he sleep. You and Mr. Lipek sleep togeth."

"Ooh yeah," murmurs Frankie faintly, not loud enough for her to hear. But Jimmy hears.

She pulls hard on Jimmy's ear until it becomes a pulsating red. When they get home, he goes straight to his bedroom and shuts the door.

The next morning he awakes at five without an alarm. He sits up in bed and rocks, thinking about the night before. If he had run faster, more quietly, he could have tagged Frankie and none of it would have happened. Or when his mother kept chasing, he should have kept running and laughed all the way home. Then today he could have said, "Yeah, my old lady's a rag." But it's too late.

"Fuck," he whispers. He likes the way it sounds. "Fuck, fuck, fu—"

The kitchen light flicks on and startles him. Through a crack in the door he sees his mother appear and disappear, her flat, heavy footsteps shaking the floor.

He knows she'll wake him soon for work, so he lies back and feigns sleep. Every morning she tries to get him to quit the job. "You face. Is white," she says in broken English that he's learned to hate. "Why you no stay home? Mr. Lipek find someone else." Every afternoon when she sees that he isn't sick, when she sees that he's making money, she stops complaining.

Hearing her approach, he rolls to his side, his back to the door.

"Giacomo," she whispers. "Giacomo . . . get up."

He stares at the empty bed table.

"Giacomo," she says more harshly.

He rolls out of bed. "Okay, Mama."

"Hurry—I let you sleep few minutes more."

She races back to the kitchen.

He steps outside his room to his dresser. On top of it are the clothes his mother has laid out for him: stiff blue jeans, T-shirt, sweatshirt, underwear, white socks. Next to the pile is a pair of bleached and starchy gym shoes. He changes quickly in front of the dresser and goes into the bathroom.

When he comes out, breakfast is ready. The smell of fried egg nauseates him, but he knows he won't be able to leave the house if he doesn't eat. Mr. Liptak will pick him up in a few minutes, so he has to hurry.

"No eat so fast, you get sick. He wait." She begins to wash the greasy pan and dishes, her movements quick and abrupt, as if she is on an assembly line and needs to finish before another stack of dishes appears. She is small and stout, with thick calves and wide feet. Even at this hour she wears black, as she has been since her aunt in Italy died over a year ago, the aunt who raised Mama after her own mother had died. Without turning she says, "When he come—tell I need three doz of eggs."

He continues to rush his food down, hoping Mr. Liptak won't be late.

"I need two gallon milk too."

"Yes, Mama."

She races into the bathroom and comes back with the clothes he has thrown into the hamper. Taking out the wooden washboard beneath the sink, she positions it at an angle in the basin. Her whole body becomes a smooth piston, her small, powerful hands rhythmically kneading the clothes across the hard ridges, her elbows bending and pushing, bending and pushing. She's fond of claiming that she gets the clothes cleaner than the white washer in the corner, an older model with rollers on top that wrings clothes through—the only part of the machine she has any use for.

Jimmy hears the familiar creak of the truck and pulls a napkin across his mouth. He gets up to leave. "I'm going, Mama."

"Wait—wait—you lunch." With wet hands she pushes the small brown bag into his chest. "Tell three doz eggs—two gallon o milk."

"Yes, Mama."

He walks out. Mr. Liptak is already across the street with four big cartons hanging from his arms. Jimmy hops onto the truck and slides open the doors to the freezer. A thick cloud of frost stings his face as he reaches in. He quickly slams the door shut and rushes back to his house, quietly setting down the milk and eggs behind the screen.

As he eases the screen shut, he looks down. On the stoop is a baby bottle. He picks it up and rips off the note attached to it and unfolds it: "Jockomoe, you and LipDick can suck on this." He folds the note and slides it into his pocket. No one will ever see it. He looks down at the bottle and starts shaking. The liquid inside is yellow. He picks up the bottle with the tips of his fingers and wipes his hands on his back pockets. He races to the alley behind the house and buries the bottle deep in a trash can. He runs to the truck, where Mr. Liptak is waiting.

"Taking out the garbage, Jim?"

"Uh-huh," says Jimmy, out of breath.

"That's a good boy. You never had to tell my boys to take out the garbage."

"Is that right?" asks Jimmy absently. He looks down the row of boxlike two-flats that line the short block, down to the schoolyard at the corner.

"Why, sure. They were always helping around the house. In fact, Bill used to help me on the truck when he was about your age."

"How old?" Jimmy knows a simple question will keep him talking for a while. He fingers the note in his pocket.

The truck eases forward.

"Oh, he was about eleven or twelve. He hated stairs, too, when he started. He would take his handkerchief and wrap it around the handles of the bottles . . ."

The truck crawls past the schoolyard, past the homerun fence. Beyond the fence, on Grand Avenue, is Jean's coffee shop, one of the last stops of the day. The schoolyard will be filled by then.

"Why don't we deliver to Jean's now?" asks Jimmy.

Mr. Liptak laughs. "Jean won't know how much she'll need until noon."

"Maybe we could—"

"Actually, years ago I delivered to Jean's at ten, ten thirty, but once Bill started working . . ."

The truck turns east down Grand. Jean's yellow sign appears in the rearview mirror on Jimmy's side. He watches until it becomes a pinpoint. As they pass Battiste's Fish Market and Vitucci Funeral and D'Amato's Bakery, his eyes glaze over.

He turns to Mr. Liptak and wants to yell, "I don't care about years ago." He wants to scream, "Why did you ever hire me? Why did you pick me? It's your fault. I could have stayed out later last night if I didn't have to work." But he says nothing.

He hasn't forgotten that he volunteered for the job. Mr. Liptak delivers milk to St. Columbkille every Monday and Wednesday. One day he came into the seventh grade homeroom to talk about the job. Only Jimmy and another boy showed any interest. Mr. Liptak picked him when he found out he was an altar boy, which Jimmy wanted to quit—almost everyone quits after sixth grade—but his mother wouldn't let him after her aunt died.

He volunteered, he admits to himself, but if Mr. Liptak hadn't walked into homeroom that morning, there would be no note in his pocket. He wants to flash the note in front of him, to underline Lip-Dick. The name suddenly fits perfectly. Almost every kid at school pronounces it "Lip-Dick," but Jimmy never paid attention. It had nothing to do with him—until now. Whenever they cut into Liptak, they'll cut into him, too, now.

Jimmy studies him. It has never occurred to him how ugly he is. His jowly, pockmarked face jiggles with each bump. His thick lips are always wet, almost drooling. Every few seconds, it seems, he stuffs his pink, bulbous nose into an enormous gray handkerchief and blows until his face is inflamed. Long strands of stringy brown hair are pasted across the top of his balding head in perfect arcs. His brows are thick, the skin beneath swollen.

Jimmy decides he is going to quit. Today. As soon as they're finished at Jean's. He'll be able to stay out after dark on Fridays.

Even his mother can stop complaining for good. He draws in a deep, settling breath and lets it out slowly.

Throughout the morning, all he can think about is what to do when they get to the schoolyard. He wants to go home and avoid everyone for a while, give them time to forget about the night before. But that might give them more time to talk about it. He could join them, laugh at their jokes, but he would need to joke back, and he can never think of what to say on the spot.

What would Frankie or Joey do? He can't even imagine. They would never work for LipDick. Or let their moms make them look like idiots. They would have kept running last night and laughed. They always know what to do.

At noon they pull up in front of Jean's. Joey and Frankie and Nino are in the field playing fast-pitch against three sixth graders.

Mr. Liptak goes in to check inventory. Jimmy jumps off and heads straight for the back of the truck. He flings open the heavy doors. Jean always orders big on Saturday, so he has to move milk crates from the front of the truck to the back, get them ready for unloading. He hops up and begins stacking crates four high. As he finishes his first stack, he hears Joey: "She was ripping into him—Cummings looked like a sack of shit . . . no, man, nothing." He strains to hear more but all he can make out is "Milkboy." It's a new word, and they play with it.

He begins stacking crates again, working quickly. As he finishes his second stack, a face appears between the bottom crates. It's Frankie.

"Hey, Jimmy. How about you let me have a pint of chocolate milk?"

"Yeah, sure." Jimmy tries to calm himself. He puts the pint down between the two crates and pushes it forward with his foot. He notices Nino and Joey sitting on the curb and puts down two more pints. "For Nino and Joey," he says.

"Hey, thanks, man."

Jimmy doesn't know what else to say, so he turns and walks to the front for another crate. As he reaches down, the doors crash shut—the lock rattles—everything goes black.

He freezes—too scared to move—crouches into a ball, feels the floor. He looks around frantically but can see nothing, not even his hand.

He crawls to the back of the truck, finds the doors, and gropes for a handle. There is none. He turns to the front of the truck. His eyes are beginning to adjust. A tiny crack of light squeezes through the sliding doors. He crawls toward it.

He wedges the tips of his fingers between the doors and works to pry them apart. They won't budge. He feels for a handle. There has to be one. He remembers the sticker on the other side of the door: EASY-OPEN DOOR. *How can I be trapped?*

He crouches down again, rubbing his arms. He has never felt so cold.

Mr. Liptak will be back soon. He can't panic.

But Mr. Liptak will see the door shut and look for him inside the store. He has to let him know he's in the freezer. He crawls to the back of the truck, raises his fist to bang on the doors, then suddenly stops.

Frankie and Nino and Joey are outside. When they hear him banging, they'll laugh. If they see that he's scared they'll never forget.

This is his chance. They'll get tired of the joke soon, open the doors, see him sitting casually on an empty crate drinking chocolate milk in the cloudy freezer—*where's the chocolate milk, I have to find it*—and then they'll laugh together—the milk has to be near, he can't be crawling when the doors open. *No more Milkboy*—

The lock suddenly rattles, and the shackle creaks open. No time to find the milk or crate. He gets out of his crawl and sits, trying not to look cold.

The door eases open, letting in a shower of light, in harsh bursts. Jimmy turns away blinded. He wants to lunge out the open door toward the light, but he can't see; he'd have to crawl. So he waits.

When his eyes adjust, he stands, walks to the back, and jumps off. He looks down at the curb. No one. He turns right.

Mr. Liptak, lock and key in hand, is staring at him, his mouth hanging open. "How in the world did—"

Jimmy turns to the schoolyard steps. They're all there, watching him: the Milkboy. He turns to the truck. There's an empty, metal crate in the back. He grabs it, hurls it like a grenade to the front of the truck where it crashes against the sliding doors.

A loud hiss shoots out. Stunned, Jimmy peers inside. Above the doors, a stream of white foam sprays out violently from a copper tube, blanketing the cartons beneath it.

Jimmy's heart sinks. He knows now what keeps the freezer

cold, what gives the freezer its rusty, metal smell. He turns. Mr. Liptak gazes helplessly at the spray, which begins now to sputter and cough. His eyes slide down to his milk and eggs, his creased face full of worry—worry, Jimmy guesses, about how he will finish his deliveries.

Jimmy's stomach tightens. The noon sun sends flashes through his chilled body. He mouths words but nothing comes out. Mr. Liptak lets out a long sigh, as if the sputtering and coughing from the copper tube have punctured and deflated him. Jimmy wants to take it back: the crate, the mean thoughts, the name LipDick. Suddenly it's the only thing that matters to him, the guys on the stairs with their legs up and their chocolate milk now distant and small.

Sulfur Memories

MICHELINO

WHEN WE WERE TEENAGERS, MY LITTLE brother Jimmy would blow things up around the schoolyard in the summer. He'd wedge a firecracker or two in the hole of one of Papa's scratched-up opera records, set it atop a trash can, light the wick, and stand back to watch the vinyl shatter and float down like black pollen. Or he'd take a glazed bismarck and turn it into an exploding birthday cake, the yellow cream flying out in fountainlike arcs. A halved soda can sandwiched around a cherry bomb was never as dramatic, but I always liked the tinny boom as the top half blasted twenty feet in the air and sailed to the ground, wisps of smoke trailing behind.

Arms folded, trying to look like the stern older brother, I'd stand at the top of the school's granite steps as things blew up around me. If I thought of some variation, like flinging the record at the sky or sticking an egg in the pop can, I kept it to myself.

One time I found him on our screened back porch unraveling

firecrackers, pouring gunpowder into a small cardboard tube, something that would hold a stack of quarters. Bent over the container, his brow pinched in concentration, he looked like a chemist, the powder spilling out in hourglass precision between the folds in the paper. When no more came out, he tapped the top of the firecracker, pulled and dropped the wick into the tube, and rubbed the tips of his fingers, trying to wipe away any excess. But no matter how much he rubbed, his fingers remained stained with this sparkling gray coat of paint dust. When the container was finally filled, he packed it down gently with the grip of a small screwdriver, slipped a thick, leathery wick inside the tube, and melted candle wax over the top. Though I doubted it would work, my legs felt weak. It was double the size of an M-80.

"What do you think you're doing?" I said.

He smirked. "Homework. What do you think?"

Having built a bomb, he must have thought he was in charge. "You little asshole," I said. I snatched the bomb and stuck it in my pocket.

"Hey—" He jumped up. "Give it back."

"Give what back?"

And then we pushed each other around a while, getting gunpowder all over our white T-shirts.

He wouldn't talk to me for a couple of weeks after that, not until the day we heard that Johnny Kessler and his brother and someone else we didn't know were at the hospital after a pipe bomb they'd been making exploded in their faces, bits of metal melting into their skin. The doctors had to use surgical tweezers to pry out about a hundred pieces just from their chests. I didn't even want to know about their faces.

"Did you hear?" I asked Jimmy.

"Yeah. So?"

"The pipe burned holes right into them," I said. I milled around, waiting for some gratitude. After all, I'd saved him from the same fate.

He glanced at me, then at the door. Dead pan, he said, "Mine was made out of cardboard, asshole."

New Neighborhood

GIACOMO

IT WAS ONE MONTH BEFORE MY fourteenth birthday. All I could think of as we drove to my new house was my name. Giacomo. It was what my aunts and uncles called me, what Mama bellowed from our back porch when she wanted me to come home. "Giaaacomo." My older brother, Michael, would call me Jock or Jockstrap or Jimmy. Most everyone else in the neighborhood called me Jockmo, which was the worst. "Yeah, Jockmo's a good boy," the adults would say. At the schoolyard, my friends, when introducing me to a new kid on the block or a cousin staying over, always felt compelled to add, "This is Jockmo, he don't swear." No one ever believed it. "No shit—you're thirteen and you don't cuss? Never?" I'd smile, hoping they would change the subject, thinking, That's right, I don't swear, motherfucker.

But all that would change. As we got farther and farther from my already old neighborhood, I stared at the back of the moving truck, the door rattling wildly with each bump. I rehearsed what I would say. "I'm Jim," I would say. Jim. Sophisticated. Cool. "Sure is fucking hot out today, isn't it?"

It took only a day or two for the cussing to sound natural to me. After all, I'd been swearing in my head for years. My new name, however, took longer to get used to. The problem was that I'd be Jim in the neighborhood, but still Giacomo or Jockstrap at home. When my aunts and uncles called and said, "*Ciao,* Giacomo," my first reaction was that they had the wrong number. They suddenly seemed so old, out of it. Even my brother couldn't handle my coolness. He'd answer the phone, "Ooooooh, it's for Jim, or should I say, James."

But none of my friends laughed. After only a week I felt more at ease than in my old neighborhood. The one person I hadn't proven my coolness to was Nick Santini. He was spending the summer in Italy with his family, but his name always seemed to pop up in conversation, like he was a neighborhood hero. It became eerie to me, almost as if he were there, as if I knew him.

"Yeah, remember the time Nicky climbed to the top of the school," someone said. "He was hanging on to one of those long-assed gutters, the downspout part, and all of a sudden it ripped away from the school. We saw him falling, man. The whole gutter started swinging away from the school, you know, like a ladder, and there's Nicky, still hanging on to it. Man, you should've seen his face."

But somehow he suffered only a few bruises.

"How many push-ups did Nicky do in gym last year? Three hundred? Yeah, three hundred something. No shit."

When I finally met him, he was shorter than I had pictured. And his face wasn't as sharply cut as I had imagined. He looked like a baby-faced Jimmy Cagney with light skin and sandy hair. Even his muscles weren't as finely toned as others had led me to believe. Yet he had square shoulders and solid arms and he always took off his shirt to remind everyone.

One day we were sitting around in front of Luigi's house. Luigi's famous dago tees and grapefruit-sized pot belly made him look, in an odd way, like one of our fathers. He *was* older than the rest of us—he'd flunked third grade several times—yet his squeal of a laugh and his tendency to holler *Yo* at unpredictable times made him seem several years younger. He was keenly aware of the rivalry between Nicky and another sinew-head on the block, Eddie Dobinski. One sunny July afternoon he suggested that the two of them have a weight-lifting contest. Nicky sauntered next door to get his bar; Eddie crossed the street and returned with his weights. They would take turns lifting, they agreed, adding five pounds each time. It became clear almost immediately that they were evenly matched. After a while, his face flushed, his back wet with sweat, Nicky ordered, "Add twenty." Luigi started hooting and yelping like a dog and quickly complied.

Nicky reached down for the bar, let out a strained shriek as he came up, and lifted it high over his head. He made it look easy. Suddenly one end of the bar began to sag. His legs became wobbly. We stood there frozen, our mouths hanging open. Nicky would straighten it out—this was Nick. He looked at the bar, his cheeks puffy and engorged, and then collapsed to the ground, flat on his back, the bar crashing to the concrete. Like a cat, however, he sprang to his feet. Everything was all right, we thought—until we looked at his wrist. It was crushed, out of joint, his hand set at an impossible angle from his arm.

I dashed across the street to call paramedics, my heart racing. I had never seen a broken bone before. When I got back to Luigi's house, Nicky was clearly worried, but he still broke out in his assured grin. He wondered if he should pull on his hand to pop it back in place. Luigi, of course, encouraged this, which made Nicky realize how stupid the plan was. We all paced, waiting to hear a siren. In the meantime, they bantered back and forth, counting all the other bones Nicky had broken. I listened, a bit in awe at their calm.

Except for Luigi, we each soon became a freshman. That was bad enough. But before I moved, I had registered at Gordon Techni-cal Catholic, my brother's school. My friends, naturally, would go to the neighborhood school, Steinmetz, Hugh Hefner's alma mater, I learned. The irony was clear to me: Gordon Tech had all boys; Stein-metz had girls and Hugh Hefner.

At the beginning of the summer, I had felt like I was on the side-lines, listening to reminiscences. And it didn't bother me. I hadn't been a part of their past. Now when their stories didn't include me, I wasn't even a part of their present. I was missing out. I could only imagine what Mr. Tamborelli's toupee looked like, or how Mr. Horton strained his neck while teaching chemistry to peek up girls' dresses. And I longed to see Diane's long legs and Wanda's huge chest.

By the end of freshman year, I was ranked nineteenth out of

about six hundred students. I doubt that any of my friends knew this, probably because I offered few glimpses into my school life. I guess I worried that they might start introducing me by saying, "This is Jim, he goes to Gordon." And the natural reply would be: "Gordon? That's Catholic, ain't it? You gonna be a priest?" Or worse: "Gordon is all boys, ain't it? What, you like boys?"

I transferred to Hugh Hefner High the next year. My sophomore ranking was 54 out of 500 students. It dropped to 94 by junior year and 140 by senior year. I suppose my plummet, though I didn't see it like that back then, had something to do with girls in my classes— not that I went out with many—but I was easily distracted, which was as good an excuse as any. Maybe it had something to do with the school. It wasn't challenging me. Maybe my new name changed something inside. Or, most likely, since Luigi and Eddie and Nicky didn't care much about school, neither did I.

The Day of Settlement

WHEN JIM CUMMINGS SAW HIS MOTHER enter Connie's Good Food, he nearly made the mistake of getting up to greet her. Instead, he turned away, buried his head in his chicken soup, and sipped quietly. He breathed in the steam, blew out, watched the noodles swirl to the sides of the bowl, stirred it deliberately. The soup, he thought, was not as good as his mother's. He wondered if she would be more upset knowing that he was cutting sixth-period biology or knowing that he was eating canned soup. His eyes slid up warily. When she started for the other dining area, he wiped his mouth and slunk outside, making sure to stuff the unpaid lunch tab into his pocket. And it would remain unpaid, he thought. He hadn't finished his soup, and they could serve his sandwich to someone else.

From his fenderless Ford Fairmont, which he figured she hadn't spotted or she would have chased him around the tables, he peered inside the restaurant. Mama sat with her back to him, across from a man wearing a dark suit. He hadn't noticed her walk in with anyone. The man was about forty-five and had stark black hair slicked straight back, receding in the front. Penciled onto his upper lip was a thin black mustache that made his mouth look pursed and tiny. His smooth hands, adorned with rings, gestured with elegant ease. He looked Italian, probably spoke it fluently and precisely, thought Jim, like they do in Rome, like they teach in school. He wouldn't use the guttural dialect of the *paese* where Jim's mother and father came from.

Jim decided he was a real estate broker. His mother had been urging his father for years to reopen his own barber shop instead of working for Bruno's his whole life. His father complained one year that the rent would be too high, another year about licenses. Finally, over the past few months, she had called several brokers for information. Jim was surprised that she was already beyond the information-over-the-phone stage.

He pulled out of the parking lot and headed back toward school, thinking how strange it was seeing his mother in a restaurant. She existed in their kitchen, pulling lids off steaming pots, or in the basement, adding detergent to the washer, or in the backyard garden, bending to pick tomatoes. She vaguely existed at work—he had seen the factory, called her there several times. But she was out of place here. He had seen her in a restaurant once—when she and his father had celebrated their fifteenth wedding anniversary—and even that had seemed peculiar. She always insisted on cooking. Going to a restaurant was an insult to her.

If he were a Realtor, Jim wondered, why wouldn't she just go to his office? Why lunch? He turned the car around. His mother got only thirty minutes for lunch, and the factory was over three miles away.

He eased into Connie's lot, parked behind another car, and looked inside. His mother and the man were gone. They probably went to look for storefronts, he thought.

As he drove back to school, his curiosity turned to suspicion. He spat out the window, the tinny taste of soup repulsing him. He spat again.

It began to dawn on him that maybe the man's name was Mario Valicchi. The long lunch break began to make more and more sense. Other events became clear. There were the phone calls, where she would pull the tangled cord onto the back porch and ease shut the kitchen door behind her; the Christmas card sent to her the last few years, signed by Mario Valicchi. Every year she would hang the card on the wall with the others. His father had seen it the first year and asked, "Lucia, who is this Mario Valicchi?" She had reacted angrily— not toward his father—but that a card was sent to her by this man whom she did not know. Had she not looked inside that first year? Or did she tape the card up to belittle her husband, her own private joke? His father never mentioned the card again, and Jim wondered now if his father had ever suspected anything.

He guessed not. His father rarely questioned his mother or defended himself from her attacks. He was a talker, she complained. He talked while others worked and made money. If only she had married Abruzzo, she always protested, she would have three houses by now. Her tirades seemed more pronounced during dinner, as if she were suggesting that they should be eating better. She lectured, between passing steaming red sauce and green salad, that back in Italy, Jim's father would often neglect to charge his customers, that he preferred instead to maintain their empty-handed patronage, their camaraderie. His business then had been a farce, she said. They lived with her father, and his shop was in the basement, next to the wine barrels. When she found out that he didn't charge everyone, she threatened to tell her father. But she never said anything. Instead, she insisted that he cut women's hair too, a decision, according to her, which allowed them to save enough money to come to America, a decision according to his father, that reduced him to a beautician.

Jim arrived at school late for his next class and decided to cut that one too. He drove around a while through the industrial park near the school, swerving to hit pot-holes, before finally heading home. He waited in the kitchen, drumming the table with his fingers, wondering if his mother would arrive at the usual time, and surprised when she did.

"You go to school today?" she asked. She wore a black skirt and satiny black blouse, the same kind she'd worn since her aunt, the one who raised her, had died. Jim studied her face, as if for the first time. It seemed strangely youthful: pear-shaped, with high cheek-bones and a generous mouth, even teeth. Her big, coffee-brown eyes seemed to glimmer.

"Uh-huh. Did you go to work?"

"You crazy. I work every day." She threw her purse on the kitchen counter and washed her hands. Without drying them she opened the refrigerator and began filling the counter with onions and lettuce and carrots.

"Is Papa going to open a new shop soon?"

"Yeh," she snickered. "He open in his sleep."

"Did you talk to any Realtors this week?" he said flatly. A tassel of hair fell over one eye, but he left it.

"I no talk." She broke apart the lettuce with her hands.

He leaned against the refrigerator, his eyes downcast. "How was lunch today, Mama?"

She stopped for an instant and glanced at him. He peeked up like he'd done hours earlier at the restaurant.

"Lunch?" she said, her brow furrowed. She turned back to the lettuce and rinsed it. "Is four clock. You hungry? I make ready soon."

"No, I'm not hungry at all, Mama." He tapped his foot. He wanted to say, "How's Mario?" but knew he wouldn't.

"No hungry. You eat by school, huh? French fry?"

He kicked lightly at the linoleum floor, making squeaks with his sneakers.

"What's wrong?" she said. "You no look good. Eh you need haircut. How many time I tell Papa to cut." She flung the carrots into the sink, and they rattled like thunder. "He no work home, he no work by Bruno."

Jim usually became just as irritated with his father's lack of ambition, but he felt a new sense of kinship with him. He said, "What do you mean he doesn't work by Bruno's? He works every day."

"He sit every day. Eh talk."

"You gotta give him a chance."

"Chance! When I come to America—"

"I know, I know. You found him a shop," he said, hoping this would stop her.

"I find shop eh I . . ."

She recounted the familiar story about how she came to America alone while Papa stayed behind to work in the basement. When he joined her a month later she had rented a small apartment with a storefront and had had CUMMINGS BARBER SHOP painted on the huge picture window. She insisted that Cummings was a better business name than Comingo. After a year they could barely pay rent, he insisting that not enough contacts had been made beforehand, she complaining that he should have worked harder to find contacts.

Until now, his mother's solitary voyage had never seemed peculiar to Jim. He had always admired her strength. She did what needed to be done. But he suddenly felt like he'd been groping wide-eyed through a pitch-dark room and finally, his eyes were adjusting. He felt his arms go cold.

He said slowly, "When you got here—to America—weren't you pregnant?"

"What?"

"What month did you get here?"

She began to chop the carrots with a butcher knife as long as her arm, sweeping the cut pieces into the sink. "I no rememb," she said, her voice trailing off. "Aprile . . . May."

"So you were pregnant?"

She waved the question away. "I no rememb."

Jim shook his head in disbelief, rolled his eyes, hoping she'd notice. He was born in September. His mother had crossed an ocean bearing him, her child, and now she claimed she couldn't remember.

He opened the refrigerator and pulled out a can of his father's beer. It trembled in his hand. He ignored his mother's curious glances and stared at the blue ribbon on the wet can. He could picture his father's dark fingers around the ribbon and hear his soft-spoken, gravelly voice as he told his stories—not at home, like Mama, but at the park, at night under the stars, the crickets humming fiercely. Jim remembered now the story of *"il giorno di liquidazione,"* the day of settlement, the day that Jim's two grandfathers formally arranged the wedding between their son and daughter. It was the first time that Jim's mother and father had met. Even as a boy, while listening to the story, Jim felt his father's uneasiness about the arrangement, as if his father were an intruder on his own engagement day.

Jim stood there brooding, thinking of a way to hurt her. He pushed his back against the refrigerator.

"I'm going to move out, Ma."

She peeled the onions. "You go out?"

"I'm moving out."

"You move out?" She turned to him and smiled broadly. "In alley?"

"I'm going to get an apartment."

"Apart-ament?" she said loudly, her face becoming flushed.

He breathed in, his chest heaving. "That's right," he said.

"You crazy." She shook her head. Tiny bits of foam started forming at the tight corners of her mouth. "You crazy. No money. You have job one month. Who pay apart-ament?"

"I'm not going to go to college in September. I'm going to work."

"What?" she said, squinting, the creases around her eyes becoming stiff.

"Not. Going. To. College. Going to work."

"Okay—no school—work. But you stay. Save money. Why you give money to apart-ament?"

"I want to be on my own."

She cursed the sky with her hands. "You crazy. You make me crazy."

"I want to be on my own. I don't want to stay here anymore."

"No talk to me," she said, her eyes welling up. She pulled a package of red meat out of the refrigerator, ripped off the plastic, and pounded the meat with a metal cleaver.

"Don't cook for me," he said.

She kept pounding, not hearing.

"Don't cook for me," he said louder. He would ruin her dinner just as she had ruined his lunch. "I have to go look at a few apartments."

She stopped and turned to him. "You seventeen," she said sharply. "No give apart-ament to you."

"They'll give. You pay and they'll give." He knew he was killing her, and amazed that he could be so cruel.

"Why you no wait?" she pleaded. "When you marry you go."

"What does that mean?"

"What?"

"What does marriage mean?"

"You find a girl. Live together."

"No, what does marriage really mean?"

"You find a girl. Live together."

"That's it?"

"You crazy." She wiped her eyes. "No talk to me."

"Okay, I won't talk to you—but I'm still moving out."

She looked up. "Why now?"

He didn't say anything for a long while. He watched the cleaver. "Everybody's got to be on their own sometime."

"I know. I know. When you marry is time."

"No," he yelled. "I'm ready now. You left when you were ready. I'm ready now."

She was crying now. "I leave because no work."

"Oh, no," he said. He looked down at the beer can. "You came here to get away from your father."

"What?" she said shrilly.

"You came to get away from your father," he said firmly, something in his chest twisting tightly, sucking the breath out of him.

"You really crazy." She started pounding the meat again, faster, as if late for an appointment.

"I know I'm right."

"Shut up."

He imagined his grandfather flinging china at the oven after hearing that he wouldn't be able to see his grandson. "You wouldn't even wait till I was born, so he could see me."

"Shut up."

"Fine."

He marched to his room and dug out his old suitcase from deep within the closet. His mother had bought it for him when he was eight, the only time he'd visited his grandfather. He remembered him as a husky man with coarse, white hairs shooting out of his nose and ears. He seldom talked, but when he did, he yelled and waved his hands frantically. One morning when Jim sat outside the farmhouse breaking walnuts with a stone, his grandfather came out of the barn with a rusty pair of scissors the size of hedge clippers. His steps were usually heavy, but he walked gently and secretly. He got behind some chickens that were tottering around freely and bent down slowly. As he reached to snatch one by the neck, they all scattered like magnets repelled. He raced around with bent knees until he finally got close enough to pounce on one. He picked it up by the stringy neck and brought it to a bucket near the barn. In one moment, the chicken squawked and rustled violently. In another, his mouth was pried open and his body forced still from hard pressure on his neck. His grandfather wriggled the rusty scissors into the narrow beak and snapped hard. Blood gushed out bright red into the bucket, tiny drops splashing onto his grandfather's face and arms, and the chicken went limp in his huge hands. His grandfather looked down at his red-speckled arms and, like a cat, wiped clean a few of them with his tongue. Jim remembered running into the field and letting loose his breakfast onto the black dirt.

His mother had traveled thousands of miles, crossed an ocean to get away from this man, Jim thought. Not only did he pick her husband, but perhaps he prevented her from marrying someone she really loved back then. Maybe Abruzzo with his three houses. Whoever it was, she loved him; Jim was sure of it somehow. And he guessed that his steel-gripped grandfather knew about the man.

Jim zipped the packed suitcase and left it on the bed, dismissing the absurd notion that maybe he was a bastard. He walked out of his room, out of his house, the screen door banging shut behind him. He knew he wouldn't be moving out right away—maybe the end of summer, maybe forget about college—but he wanted his mother to see the suitcase. It was spiteful, he knew, but he couldn't stop himself.

As he stormed down the street, tears began to well up in his eyes, and the street seemed to shimmer, like after a cooling rain. His mother never did get away from her father, Jim thought; her marriage was a constant reminder. He understood. But he would never allow anyone to cheat him like that. He wasn't raised on a simple, back-assed farm. He would get away. And he'd make sure that others treated him fairly. He would make sure.

Confidences

NINE YEARS AFTER OPENING HIS OWN barber shop, ten months before his wedding day, arranged by his father—"After all, you're twenty-eight; it is time," his father flatly insisted—Fabio Comingo betrayed a shop confidence. At first he convinced himself that what he did was an extension of that confidence, that he was acting in the interests of his good customer, Pietro Ungaretti. But it was not long before he berated himself, admitting whose interests he was serving.

"If I could only speak with her," Pietro said, this after weeks of lamenting about the shortage of women at work at the police station in Naples. Fabio had understood his anguish but was slightly appalled by the supply-and-demand nature of the complaint. So when Pietro mentioned a longing for a particular girl, Fabio could not help but feel amused. He was tempted to say, "Ah, yes. She would make a good investment for any man." But, as usual, he smiled placidly and said nothing.

Pietro straightened his back and rolled his neck around like a tortoise as Fabio slapped white powder on his neck. "So what do you think?" Pietro asked.

Fabio offered him a mirror.

"No no no, I mean about Serafina?"

Serafina had been a childhood friend of Fabio's younger brother Miguel. When he thought of her, he still pictured uneven brown bangs and a gap-toothed smile.

"She is a fine girl," Fabio said. He meant to say *woman,* but *girl* slipped out. Either way, this was not what Pietro wanted to hear, Fabio knew.

"If only I could . . ." Pietro tapped on the arms of the leather chair with his palms, as if deliberating some master plan.

But he was simply waiting, Fabio was sure. Well, Fabio could wait, too. It was his shop, after all. In the end, of course, he relented and promised to speak with Serafina.

A LITTLE AFTER NOON THE MEN came as usual. They left their farms when the sun was harshest and gathered at Fabio's, largely ignoring him, not resentfully or patronizingly, but as a group ignores a priest, with measured deference, intent on enjoying their shade, some wine, and their hearty bantering. These were the essentials, Fabio knew. Rarely did they even ask for haircuts at these times. Only later, when they visited Fabio alone, did they sit in the chair. Then the shop was transformed into what Fabio liked to think of as his confessional, where customers offered glimpses into their tangled lives and where Fabio helped to restore a semblance of order to the mess.

There was nothing remarkable about himself, Fabio admitted, other than, as he discovered early in his career, the way he knew when to offer reassurances of confidence. "The walls here are thick, insulated" he would say, and pat the back of the chair. "No sounds escape." And, again unremarkable, there was the snapping of the crisp apron as the patron settled himself in the chair, the rhythmic *snip-snip* of the beveled blades, the whisk of the brush against the back of the shaved neck, the powders, the shaving creams. These things in their precision worked their magic. These things instilled calm. Even the shop itself played its part. Soon after he opened it, a barn really, built by his father and brother nine years ago, Fabio removed all the mirrors. He convinced his father and brother to cut out more windows so customers could admire the blue range of the Apennines rather than tufts of hair tumbling down an apron. When Fabio gazed out the windows at a clearing through the cluster of cypresses and towering pines, he could glimpse the Appian Road at the spine of the hills, track it as it wound around rolling green and brown valleys. In school they taught him that the apostle Paul had escaped arrest using this very road, that Mark Antony journeyed hundreds of miles over it to court Cleopatra, and Fabio often imagined boarding a bus one day and *being* at that spot that he spied from the shop window, looking up at the smattering of familiar roofs in the hills, already missing the small town, yet feeling a stranger to it.

* * *

"DID YOU COLLECT ANY MONEY TODAY?" Santo Comingo wanted to know, his father's first question each day after work.

Fabio turned the flame down under the pot of boiling water. "Three customers," he said. This didn't include the few lire that the noon patrons left for wine and espresso.

"Not bad," Santo said.

But not good—which didn't matter. Their real money came in from the tomatoes and corn and heads of lettuce in the field that his father and brother planted, busheled, and sold. And tobacco. Especially tobacco. No one else in the village was willing to take the time to cultivate the soil, to pick and cure and age the leaves. It was Fabio's job, as it had been since his mother died in childbirth with Miguel, to run the house. Though he resented the notion that he had become the mother of the family, Fabio could not deny its accuracy. Even now, he could not help but compare his father's leathery hands and arms, bronzed, enriched from the sun, to his own smooth, fish-belly-white skin. And although he had his father's long, angular face, it wasn't as chiseled or as sun-creased as his father's.

When his father pulled off one of his mud-caked boots and dropped it to the ceramic kitchen floor, Fabio felt tempted to reprimand him. Instead he said, "Do you know, Papa, if Serafina Candoressi still mends pants?"

Without looking up, his father rubbed his foot. He slid off the other boot and flung it to the floor, chunks of clayed earth splattering like glass. He stripped off his soiled socks, discarded them next to the boots, and hobbled to the bathroom, where he would soak his feet.

"I do not concern myself with such foolishness," he said, his voice trailing off. "Mending . . . Ha!"

Over the sound of running water, through the closed door, Fabio could still hear a muffled, "How would I know about Serafina?"

Fabio's hands trembled as he placed a fistful of spaghetti into the pot. "Imbecile," he whispered. He fought back the urge to slam the pot to the floor, to watch the scalding water curl around the mud and slip under the bathroom door. He thought of storming out of the house, but dismissed the idea immediately, deciding that this was not what twenty-eight-year-old men do.

As he mulled over what men do, he pushed the stiff stalks of spaghetti down into the boiling water, admonishing himself for using such a small pot, thinking that what men surely do *not* do is cook.

In order to calm himself, he shifted his rage from his father to other, safer targets; it had become a deliberate pattern for him, a ploy. It is Mama's fault, he thought: She should have insisted on the hospital sooner rather than relying on the stupid, fumbling midwife. I'd be out in the fields now.

But he would not allow his anger toward his mother to fester. If he did, he knew he would become despondent for days, even though he barely remembered her. For a fleeting moment, he wondered if his father's gloomy spells were rooted in the same anger, the same guilt. Thinking of his mother, dead, and his father's grief, all he had been through, nearly always softened his rage, as it did now, though he tried this time to fight it.

And he could not forget the mangy-looking mutt whose coat he had cut when he was nine. When his father came home, he was so pleased that he sat down and instructed Fabio to cut *his* hair. Fabio dutifully complied and tried his best, but he may as well have used sheep shears. His father's head looked lopsided, cratered patches stamped along the top.

When Fabio reluctantly offered a mirror, his father barely glanced at it. "Bravo," he said. Looking back, Fabio wondered if his father saw opportunity in the cut, a chance to extract a useful service from his son. Had he not been branded a barber back then, he'd certainly be in the fields now.

SHE ANSWERED THE DOOR, PUZZLEMENT IN her eyes, and said nothing. He stared at her and seemed bewildered himself. Why have I never noticed that long neck before? Fabio wondered.

Serafina Candoressi pinched at the waist of her cream-colored cotton dress to straighten it and wiped her palms on the backs of her thighs.

"Fabio," she said. She had strong, high cheekbones and blushed, rose-petal lips. Her eyes darted around, as if she expected someone to be there with him. "Is everything— Come in."

"I can come later if this is a bad time."

She pushed her dark hair behind her shoulders where it lay like the train of a gown. He imagined taking it in his hands and combing it and— He tried to imagine more but could not. He had never barbered a woman, never had *any* training, in fact.

"No, no, come in," she said.

In his awkwardness, he was about to blurt, "I have a customer," but she said, "How is Miguel?"

"I do not see him often. He works with Papa all day," he said, and regretted it, the implied admission that he did not work the land like most of the other men. He noted her skin, as pale as his own.

She sat down on the edge of the kitchen chair, her back straight, as if to say, Well, what do you want? Why are you here? You barely nod when I see you. How dare you come to my house?

Stop this nonsense, Fabio told himself. It is no wonder you have known so few women. Fabio the barber. Fabio the priest. Was this how she saw him?

She started to get up. "Let me get you a cup of coffee."

"No, no," he said, and waved her down into the chair. He scanned the room—a china cabinet in the corner filled with gilt-rimmed plates, lace doilies set at measured distances along the walnut table— then stared at the ceiling. "Well, maybe a small cup," he said.

As she disappeared into the kitchen, Fabio sank into his seat and immersed himself in the smells of the house, this house where a woman lived. The scent of jasmine and perfume hung in the air and nearly blotted out the smell of steam shooting out from the rusty iron in the corner. This woman's house was well tended, he thought. His own house was clean, of course, nearly disinfectant clean, he made sure of that, but he could never bleach out the rank scent of butchered meat that his father hung in the cellar to dry. He could not even go down there any more. The few times that he did, as a boy, the pungent odor would catch in his throat, like it would suffocate him, and he would run out of the house fighting the urge to retch, afterward panting and spitting, bending low to wipe his spittle on the grass, breathing in the sweet scent, trying desperately to erase the meat stench. But he could not erase the image of the slaughtered hogs, skinned, hanging on a makeshift clothesline by their legs or hind or whatever was left.

Serafina sauntered back into the living room. "It will be ready in a minute," she said. She unplugged the iron and sat down. "So . . . how is Miguel?" When it registered in her eyes that she'd already asked, she tapped her forehead with her fingertips and rolled her eyes. "Where is my head?" she said.

They both laughed uneasily. He was relieved and surprised that she was as nervous as he was. In the silence that followed he realized that Miguel was their only link.

"Do you remember," he said, "when Miguel would throw stones at the lizards? He would try to cut their heads off."

"Yes," she said.

And Fabio was always disheartened by his own squeamishness, made more apparent by Serafina's intrepidness.

"He would miss every time," she said.

"Not every time," he said. Fabio remembered the heads flying one way from the force of the throw, the rest of the lizard wriggling away for what seemed a long while. He could not wait for the tail to stop.

"The head would go one way," he said and pointed.

She pointed the other way. "I know," she said. "And the tail—"

They laughed.

"That was a long time ago," she said.

He wanted to say: *It feels like I have lived my life separated like that.* It was something he might say if he were a patron in his own shop.

Another unnerving silence followed.

"Do you remember climbing the cherry tree?" she said.

"With you?"

"And Miguel."

"No."

"You *must* remember."

"I'm afraid not."

"You would always climb higher than us."

"Higher? And I would . . ." He would look down at them, not up, as he had been searching for in his memory. "So I must have been, maybe, thirteen?" Which made Miguel eight, not tall or limber enough to manage but a few short branches. But by ten, Miguel climbed so high that it must have looked to him like his older brother, Fabio, was on the ground.

"Yes, I remember now," he said. And he remembered suddenly that he did not bother with underwear back then, that he found her staring blankly from below one time as he straddled two limbs. He nearly fell off the tree trying to adjust his shorts so that they held everything in.

She got up and started for the kitchen. "You lost your balance one time, didn't you?" she said, somewhat coyly, Fabio thought.

He felt like he was in the tree again, the same catapulting surge of panic. What had been a fleeting embarrassment for him must have been an education, a first glimpse, to an eight-year-old girl, he figured. Why else would she still remember?

"How much sugar?" she called.

"Four."

As she carried the coffee to him, he decided that he could get used to this: a wife serving coffee in the afternoon. He could prepare dinner, learn to cut her hair. She set the cup and saucer down by his hand, her hair swaying in front of him. He tried to take in the jasmine scent but smelled coffee, along with something more familiar that he couldn't quite place at first. Tobacco. His father had a small field behind Serafina's house, and the aroma from the mottled green leaves had wafted in through an open window. The leaves usually seemed acrid to him, reminding him of the voracious June beetles that attacked the leaves, creating the haunting image of his father looming over him, but now, sitting close to Serafina, he breathed in the plant's sweet scent.

The next day he returned, fabricating a story about a suit whose sleeves were too long—would she tailor it? When she asked why he did not bring it, he felt caught but remembered a suit he had tried on years before in Naples and described that one. When she insisted that he bring it the next day, he admitted that he had not yet bought it, that he wanted to find a seamstress first. She grinned but said nothing. As he left her house, all he could think of was arranging a trip to the city so he could purchase his first suit.

The next morning Pietro ambled into the shop.

"These things take time," Fabio said.

"I understand," Pietro assured him, nodding, though he seemed irritated. "I will be working for the next six days. We will talk when I get back."

"I will talk with her," Fabio said. He still intended to mention Pietro's interest, but he felt a stronger urge to hand Pietro the measurements for his waist, neck, and inseam so he could bring back a suit for him.

When Pietro returned, Fabio garnered up the courage to claim that he hadn't seen Serafina. On the days that he wasn't busy, he simply could not find her, he said. Pietro gazed out the window as if looking for her, but his irritation seemed spent. He looked haggard suddenly, hunched. He had resigned himself, Fabio decided, to pursue someone else, someone up north maybe. Besides, he would be better off. What woman wanted to wait days at a time for some pistol-carrying government worker to return for what would amount to a visit each time?

"Well, when you see her then . . ."

"Of course," Fabio said.

SEVERAL WEEKS AFTER HIS INITIAL VISIT to Serafina's house, Fabio said to her, "Every time I come here, I sit in this chair."

She sat across from him in her usual spot.

"I do not strap you in," she said.

Whenever their eyes met, as they did now, they would hold for a moment, and then another, until Fabio looked away. He rarely allowed himself to look directly at her, unless she was glancing away, in which case he studied the contour of her face. During those times when their eyes did lock, her gaze was easy and penetrating, but always distant, inaccessible.

"The chair is comfortable enough, I suppose." He settled himself in the chair and looked casually beyond her toward the stairs that led up to what he imagined to be the bedrooms. "When was the last time we talked?" he said. "I mean before I showed up weeks ago."

"Without your suit?"

"Monday," he said. "I will close shop Monday. I will take the train and buy that suit."

She crossed her legs, rocked the top one, her slipper balancing on her toes. She nodded, amused. "Monday," she said.

"You will see," he said, with the right amount of bravado that he knew would please her. He was grateful that she had never pressed him about why he suddenly appeared one day, or about why he continued to visit nearly every afternoon—though he hoped that that was more or less apparent by now.

"So when was the last time?"

She shook her head. "Three years ago?"

"When your mother died," he said. "I marched through here with the others, had some coffee. I am not sure that we even spoke."

She rose, walked over to him, and collected his saucer and empty coffee cup. "We spoke," she said, her face now close to his. " 'I know what it is like not to have a mother.' That is what you said."

"One doesn't know what to say at those times," he said apologetically, leaning back.

"Oh, no. It was comforting."

She set the saucer and cup on the leather footrest by his feet and sat next to him. "So what is it like?" she said. "Not to have a mother."

"It is all I know," he said.

"What is it like?"

"I feel cheated, I suppose."

"Like she abandoned you?"

If he'd felt abandoned as a boy he couldn't remember. "No . . . I cannot explain it." He didn't want to admit his resentment at having to become the mother. And he was afraid that once he uttered his resentment, it would sound trivial.

"And for you," he said. "What is it like?"

"A relief."

"Oh." His voice trailed off. "I didn't know she was sick."

"She wasn't."

Her bluntness always made him stir. At first he suspected that she simply enjoyed shocking him, which repelled him, yet her brashness also made her sophisticated and wildly attractive to him.

"It is only lately," she said, "that I have finally admitted to my relief." She looked down, rubbed the fingers of her left hand, as if wiping them of soil, her brashness gone now. "I have never told anyone. Relief because my mother died. You must think—what I thought. That I do not deserve to live in her house. But just because I am relieved does not mean I did not love her."

"I understand," he lied.

"She would not let you breathe. If guests came and you didn't fold napkins properly, she erupted—always after everyone left, of course."

She raised her hand as if to pound a table, to emphasize a point—he imagined her doing this alone, muttering complaints— but she brought it down slowly and seemed resolved not to say more. She took in the room with a glance, as if she were a stranger in it, and Fabio finally understood the formality of their meetings. This was her mother's room, where her mother entertained. The Capodimonte statues and vases were marks of old-fashioned tastes. Serafina simply maintained the room.

He was not sure if he should tread further. "And now?" he said. "You feel more . . . what? Free?"

"Free?" she said.

She looked at him, a slow grin forming at the corners of her mouth. She fought it, covering her mouth with her fingers, a gesture he had seen her use flirtatiously. But she could not hold back the wheezing, which soon turned into a hard-edged laugh. How ridiculous, she seemed to say. Just as he began to feel that she was laughing at him, she stopped.

* * *

Fabio wished he had not overheard, as if the overhearing brought on his misfortune. As he waited at the counter of the café for his wine, peering out back to the lighted boccie alleys, listening to the *chink* of the balls as they collided and caromed, followed by the usual jeers, he heard one of the card players in front of the bar roar with laughter. At first it was part of the din, part of the back clapping, the slapping down of cards. But then he heard "barber." He held his breath, straining to hear more. "The barber makes house calls now," the voice said.

So everyone knew, or would soon know, about Serafina and him. Not that there was much to know. He hadn't so much as touched her, did not want to risk such an advance and jeopardize his welcome at her house. He anticipated his daily visits so eagerly now that even his father noticed a change and asked why he had become so sullen. When Fabio suggested to Serafina, hinted really, that he would like to see her one evening, for a walk perhaps, she deftly sidestepped the suggestion with "We will see," as if she were a mother deflecting the pleas of a child.

His father swiftly squelched the spread of house call rumors when he announced his plans for Fabio. Her name was Lucia Tegolari, he said. She lived near Salerno, came from a fine family, and would make a fine wife. He spoke as if describing a trip to the market, all the time picking at the dirt lodged beneath his fingernails the way he liked to do. You must be joking, Fabio told him. They argued for a while, what Fabio would look back on as the thirty minutes that decided his fate. Early in the argument

Fabio decided not to vent his rage, knowing he could not win that contest.

"You do not care to marry?" his father said. He spoke softly, as if trying to seem sage.

"I care to manage my own life," Fabio said.

"You can open a shop in Salerno. There will surely be more customers there. It will be a regular business."

"I have a regular business."

His father looked at him with raised brows and seemed to suppress a laugh. "A bigger business then," he said.

We should not be talking about business, Fabio thought, or arranging the lives of people as if they were a business. He drummed his fingers on the table, for a moment thinking reckless thoughts: shaving his father too closely next Sunday; eloping with Serafina. But he was not a reckless man; he felt it in him, like some rabid dog locked in the cellar of his mind, but he had never called upon it. Maybe never would. But, one way or another, he would surely not go along with this preposterous arrangement, he thought.

For the next few days Fabio anguished over how to tell Serafina, anxious to tell her soon, before she heard. It is all a mistake, I don't love her, he would say. I think of you always. When he did finally knock on her door a week later, there was little doubt that she had heard, that the entire village had heard. Customers made special trips to the shop to offer hearty congratulations. It seemed to Fabio all so calculated, as if his father had paid them to stop in. Women came with pastries and baskets of fruit. He tried to refuse the gifts, even deny the news, but they laughed and kissed his cheeks and bounced out of the shop. The well-wishers, instead of hastening a trip to Serafina's house, numbed him. He felt trapped, as if they were congratulating someone else, and before long that other person was politely thanking them and nodding.

Serafina kissed him on the cheek like the others; their first kiss, Fabio thought, not what he'd imagined it would be. He stood inside her doorway, stammering, his thoughts full of apologies.

"You look good," he said. He grabbed the sleeve of her gathered, cotton dress and rubbed it between his fingers as if he were examining the material. It would be the closest he would come to touching her, he thought. "This is the dress you wore on my first visit."

"Yes, it is," she said, smiling. "Please. Sit."

He was afraid she would respond coldly, but she was genuinely pleasant, more pleasant than usual perhaps.

"No," he said. "I came to—" What? Apologize? Elope?

"You don't need a reason to come here," she said. "Sit. For a minute."

They took their usual places, and he let out a few sighs, patted his lap with his palms, trying to steady his trembling hands.

"I wish I were more like you," he said. He'd made it clear during other visits that he admired her boldness.

"Don't," she said and shook her head. "Don't."

"You look . . . sad," Fabio said.

She forced a laugh and brought her hand to her chest, where her heart would be, he thought. "Do I?" she said.

He looked out the window, not wanting to press, to make her uncomfortable.

"I suppose I'm a bit sad," she said. "I become sad when I know that someone will not get what he really wants."

She was speaking about him, not herself. She was not losing what *she* really wanted. He felt stupid. He realized now that he had hoped she would be gravely disappointed, weeping. And he understood finally her aloofness, her casual confidence with him. She did not worry about becoming romantically entangled with him; she had someone else. He had the odd sensation of discovering something he'd known, really, all along, from the very first visit.

A MONTH OR SO LATER SERAFINA Candoressi eloped with Pietro Ungaretti and they didn't return. Serafina's father trudged into the shop stunned. Why did she need to elope? She didn't even give him a chance to consent!

By then Fabio had resigned himself to his own marriage to Lucia Tegolari, whom he'd soon meet, and felt a sort of prankish pleasure in hearing about Serafina. As he'd known all along, she was the reckless one. Still, he missed her sorely and longed to see her one last time.

When he did, shortly before his wedding day, the world had fallen off its axis. Fabio, always on the fringe, overheard. "Poor Serafina," said the old women. They huddled around each other in the cobblestone square, outside the stores in the village, moaning and whispering. When tragedy struck, these women, draped in black, came to life. Fabio assumed that Serafina's father, who had withered years after Serafina suddenly left, had died. Fabio moved closer, pretending to be interested in a sign in a window, and discovered that something—he couldn't determine what—had happened to Pietro.

He rushed back to his shop and waited for customers to pour in. They would leave the fields early for this. When they arrived they all wore solemn faces. Pietro was dead, they said, beaten by muggers as he walked home from the police station. Once they had overcome their disbelief and exhausted their lamentations, they became animated as they ballyhooed theories. The muggers, they must have been kids, punks. If only Pietro had been in uniform, they would have left him alone. If only he had worked minutes longer that day. What ill luck.

Fabio's father strolled in, but there was a slight hitch in his step. His brow seemed more furrowed than usual, his eyes bloodshot. "He arrested someone who should not have been arrested," he said.

The men stopped chattering and turned. They had not noticed him walk in. Fabio felt some consolation that these men were also intimidated by his father. Yet his father also had a way of drawing them to him.

"It has the marks of a hired hand," Santo said.

"But they beat him to death," someone said. "Why—"

"They probably just meant to hurt him." He swaggered to the barber chair. "Sometimes arrangements don't quite work out as planned."

And that would end it in his mind, Fabio thought. No grief, no lamentations. Pietro might even have deserved it.

The men cut their visit short, as they always did when his father showed up, sighing, saying they had to get back to work. Before they filed out though, they reluctantly asked if Santo knew any other facts of the murder. They wanted to hear the ugly facts. His father, of course, always seemed to know everything. The men came to Fabio to confess, to his father to draw out information.

"Here is how I understand it," Santo said, adding that Serafina's father had confided to him. "Pietro was punched in an unfortunate spot in the stomach, which made him throw up. But before he could, he was hit in the throat." He glanced over his shoulder. "Fabio, a haircut," he said. He grabbed an apron and tied it around his own neck. "He suffocated," he said.

Whatever honor Serafina had sacrificed by eloping was gained back doubly when she decided to bury her husband in the village where he was born. The usual entourage of women who showed up at times like these busied themselves in the kitchen: setting the body on the table, draining fluids from it, cleaning and dressing it. When Fabio, to his surprise, was summoned to groom the corpse, he felt revulsion, even terror, but he marched over immediately.

When he arrived, Serafina's father, pale and frazzled, greeted him and slipped out to have a smoke at the bar. Fabio walked through the familiar living room toward the kitchen. The scent of Serafina's perfume—of Serafina—stopped him and reeled him back to the chair, *his* chair, back then. He fondly remembered glancing out the window, studying the ceiling, and finally meeting her eyes, smiling at her smile. He turned. The empty wooden coffin at the end of the room steadied him.

Serafina sat in the kitchen chair, her back to her husband, who lay on the table, a crisp linen sheet covering his body. The rank smell took Fabio back and sent a flash of nausea through him. He had expected to find Pietro in his suit, lying in the coffin, prepared, done, but now realized how foolish this would be. The haircut, of course, would dirty everything. He suddenly felt awe for the women who had left.

Serafina turned in her chair and looked at him. Her eyes were dry but raw, as if she hadn't slept.

"I'm grateful," she said.

He remembered that she had thanked him for saying the right thing at her mother's wake, but he felt at a loss now. "I am glad to help," he said. "I brought—" He looked down at his paper sack of tools and pushed it out to her as if he were offering chocolates. "Scissors," he said.

A slow grin started to take shape at one corner of her mouth, but she could not sustain it. "I did not know how else to see you," she said. She looked at the bag and dismissed it with an easy flick of her wrist. "You will not need that."

It took a few moments for the words to work their way through the dense air, to take form for him. Her dismissal wasn't simply a polite reconsideration of a burdensome request. She had no intention of— He breathed a sigh of relief, as if someone had lifted a great weight off him.

"I was not sure you would come," she said.

Now that his future was certain he felt he could say anything. "If you had asked me to come to Naples I would have," he said, hoping to sound devoted. But he spoke too loudly, too casually. With measured softness now, he said, "It must have been difficult for you to come back."

"I had nowhere else to go."

There was a long pause then, and they spoke a while of burial arrangements and the church mass.

"Were you angry when I left?" she asked.

"Angry?"

"I didn't say anything. Even good-bye."

"There was no—"

"No, I should have told you."

He was pleased that she had even thought of him. He glanced at the table, wished now that he had fulfilled Pietro's request.

"Did Pietro ever mention . . . ," he said.

She laughed. And seemed embarrassed that she had allowed anything to penetrate her grief. "Yes, he told me."

"He did not resent me?"

She stared at her husband. "He said he could understand. He said, How could any man not—" Her eyes glazed over and she was somewhere else, in Naples maybe. "He loved to flatter me. He paid attention to me."

Fabio recalled all the times that he had flattered her, paid attention to her, and scolded himself for being jealous at such a time. Besides, she made it clear from the beginning, by things she did not say or ask, that she and Fabio would never do more than talk.

He moved his chair closer. "After you left," he said, "your father came into the shop." He folded his hands and gazed at a spot on the tiled floor, thinking about how to go on without prying. "He could not understand why you decided, why you did not, did not tell him."

She was suddenly flamboyant in her outrage. "He would have disapproved. He would have told me to wait for someone better." But her answer seemed rigid, rehearsed, as if she'd been expecting the question. He was sure she was lying.

She rose and shuffled to the table, stroked her husband's hair, gently running her hand from his forehead, around his ear, then down toward his neck. Over and over again.

He thought this might be his cue to leave, but suddenly her legs buckled and she collapsed onto the table, clutching Pietro's shoulders, sobbing uncontrollably, deep rattling cries.

He came up behind her, stood there soldier straight and set his hand on her back and didn't move it. When her crying subsided, Serafina rose to her feet and wiped her eyes, as if embarrassed by her display.

Shoulder to shoulder they gazed down at the table, Fabio avoiding, as he had done since he arrived, any extended glances at poor Pietro. He felt Serafina's closeness. In his mind he noted, with something like wonder, the sound of their breathing filling the room, how sometimes their breaths would sound like one as they both drew in air, and for the briefest of moments, held it, creating an absolute stillness in the room.

Fabio studied the man's face now, expecting to find bruises, swollenness, but found only what he thought was a look of anguish. The hair was lumpy and matted, longer than Pietro usually wore it, which made him look scruffy, like a vagabond.

"Will the women then . . . finish him?" he asked.

"I do not know."

He looked down at the brown bag still in his hand. It was crimped and spotted where he'd been wringing it. He unrolled the bag, careful not to tear it, and pushed his hand inside. He pulled out his comb and scissors.

He slipped around Serafina and took his place, snipping at the air like he usually did, ready to begin, but not sure how. He dropped to his knees as if praying, seeing the haircut now from something like his normal angle.

He was ready. He looked up at Serafina for consent, for encouragement even, a sign that said he was entrusted with this final touch. She moved closer and stroked Fabio's hair like she'd done earlier with her husband, and bent over to kiss him on the forehead. And with that he started.

At the wake the next day, Fabio stayed the entire evening, not caring what anyone would have to say, including his father, who arrived wearing a clean white shirt and pressed dark trousers. When Fabio spotted him, he slipped undetected into a corner of the kitchen that allowed him a view of the coffin and Serafina, who stood near it, her back to Fabio. One by one the mourners filed up to Serafina and offered condolences, promised to help in any way, then moved on to pray over the coffin. When his father reached Serafina, he stood next to her, placed his hand on the small of her back, and began to caress it. And then it happened. Serafina reached around, squeezed the burly fingers with what seemed like all her force, and removed the hand from her back. Fabio could have sworn he saw her shiver. Fabio felt lightheaded, not sure his legs would hold him. He stumbled to a chair and sat in it. This changed nothing, he told himself over and over. What did this change? He only resented that his father could still surprise him. A sardonic smile spread across his face: this was his father's wedding gift to him, was all. He pictured his father's fingers on his own back, imagined them curling around his waist. These were fingers of great strength, capable of squeezing the breath from a life, yet deft enough to inspire confidence from someone who could not know better.

When the Rains Come

WHILE EVERYONE ELSE IN THE VILLAGE prayed for rain, Lucia Tegolari thanked God for the parched earth and the near-dry wells and the billows of dust that caught in her throat as she stepped out of her stone house. When her friends could speak of nothing else but those *matti* at the aqueduct who should be so kind as to turn the water on, for at least an hour, so they, her friends, could fill their pails at the square and later bathe properly, Lucia silently cheered for the shutoff.

The same drought that had withered and baked lettuce leaves and tomato plants had sent her Rosario Antonelli each week, which had renewed Lucia. His wagon, pulled along by a myopic mule who seemed with each step ready to collapse, bounced along the narrow dirt path that led to the Tegolari farm. Lucia, bent in the field picking what remained of the string beans or checking the progress of the dying eggplants, would listen for the sluggish jostle of the wagon, the creaking wheels, then, as the wagon neared, the clomping hooves, the clanking of the bridle, and, finally, the baritone boom of Rosario as he urged the mule on.

In the wagon lay tanks filled with what Rosario claimed was *aqua virgo,* water from the legendary spring near Rome. Everyone in San Salvatore knew that the water probably came from a more proximate source, the Basilicata region perhaps, but no one disputed his claim. They knew he'd been to the university in Naples and that after his studies had returned to Faicchio, the neighboring village at the base of Mount Taburno. At first they scorned him for wasting his education, not knowing what he *had* studied, though it surely wasn't delivering water, but later became impressed that he'd returned at all, that he hadn't become elitist, which they equated with corruption. They wanted to believe he made special arrangements through contacts made up north who shipped the tanks to him by rail.

Lucia didn't care if Rosario stole the tanks, which frightened her, this new brashness in her. Each night she filled a copper cauldron with his *aqua virgo,* stepped into the basinlike tub, and let the water cascade over her, imagining Rosario's arms around her, his hands caressing her body like it had never before been touched in her seventeen years. This image sometimes became so real that she trembled.

The first time she saw him she paid little notice. Her father, who often had visitors delivering goods, asked Lucia to guide him to the small bell tower attached to the house. Rosario tagged along behind her, his whistling bouncing off rafters and echoing through the halls. She didn't recognize the song, but it sounded airy, operatic, blown out with assurance. Glancing over her shoulder she noted that, even while whistling, he seemed to be smiling. It wasn't until he climbed the belfry to check the water level, Lucia following with her eyes, that she had been struck. His khaki trousers, though rumpled and baggy, spoke of shops in Rome and Milan, sites Lucia only dreamed of. He wore a vest, unbuttoned, over his blue cotton shirt and a blue paisley handkerchief around his neck.

When he reached the top she followed him up the ladder, without hesitation, her boldness, since there was little room in the belfry for even one, shocking her.

"I understand," he said over his shoulder, "that tonight you will parade St. Francis of Paolo around the square."

"Me?" she said, short of breath, though not from the climb.

"The village, I mean."

"I suppose," she said. "Parading around a statue for rain strikes me as more an act of superstition than faith." She wanted him to know she'd outgrown the village.

He turned to her and grinned, his aquiline nose flaring out. They stood an arm's length apart. Lucia gripped one of the beams to plant herself in the spot. She would not step closer, but neither would she turn away from his gaze. His eyes were brown pools, intense. Rosario looked away and crouched low to inspect the tank, the light from the lone tower window behind him pouring down on his dark locks of hair. On a boy the short curls would have appeared foolish, clownlike, but on Rosario they seemed statuesque, like something sculpted by Michelangelo.

"It's superstition, is it?" he said, tapping the tank. "So your villagers damn themselves?"

She snickered. "I suppose we all damn ourselves in ways."

He glanced up. "And you? You have your ways?"

"I am working on them," she said. She laughed one of her father's flippant laughs. "And you?"

"Oh, yes," he said. "I have been to the university." He reared his head and let out a sardonic laugh, more natural than hers.

"You regret going?"

"No. But there is a danger, I think, in knowing too much, knowing more than one's mother and father." He peered down the ladder at the wooden floor and shook his head. "I wonder how many hundreds of times my parents' hands have blistered turning dirt, cultivating it, so their son could attend the university, and it has put a wedge between us, this education."

"It is all book knowledge," she said scornfully, trying to hide her envy. But having completed only six grades herself, she felt insulted as well. "Your university books won't tell you how to live, how to—"

"Perhaps not," he said. He put up his hand so that she would take it and steady him as he stood. The fingers were long and pink, not field hands. "Books instruct the heart," he said, still holding her hand. "It's what one of my history professors used to say."

Lucia let her fingers slip through his grip. "That may be," she said, "yet these books have placed a wall between you and your parents."

He shrugged and nodded, conceding. "When I finished school I did return. No?" He glanced below him and began to descend. "I wouldn't call it a wall between us. A high fence maybe." He stopped on the ladder and looked up at her. "But you're right. Impenetrable."

* * *

IMPENETRABLE WAS A UNIVERSITY WORD AND it stuck with Lucia even hours after Rosario departed. It resounded in her head, taunted her. It made the shelf that held the dozen dusty books her family owned seem bare and shoddy. When her father trudged in from the fields she sat in the hallway next to the kitchen poring through one of the books. Though the text was elementary, a picture book on the history of Italy, it intrigued her. She hoped it might offer a glimpse into her own heart.

"My efforts are wasted," her father announced. "If we don't get water soon . . . even the olive trees . . ." As he disappeared into the kitchen, his words trailed off and he muttered what had become his usual grunts of late. "Lucia," he called. A chair scraped against the pine floor. "Lucia."

"Papa."

"Will we eat tonight?"

She slapped the book shut and raced to the kitchen.

"Your brother will not join us for supper," he said.

She suppressed her snideness. "Is this news?" she wanted to say. Her mother's death four years ago, rather than forging them together, frayed whatever loose ties that remained. Her brother, Dominick, two years older than she, worked the farm as if it were his own, but when the day was done, he was gone.

"Maybe St. Francis will cry bucketfuls tonight," her father said, "and the tears will run down from the square into the valleys."

She glanced over to gauge his tone, thinking she'd see sarcasm in his dull gray eyes but detected no trace. Square-jawed, he stared absently out the window. Though he attended church nearly every Sunday, he was not what Lucia regarded as religious. He attended more out of single-minded obligation, like milking the cows or feeding the chickens, than spiritual zeal.

"I think I will stay home tonight," Lucia said. She had her back to him but felt his eyes. "I don't think—I'm not feeling too well."

He pushed his chair away from the table, rose slowly, and started for the door. His steps were lumbering, deliberate. "We have not had rain in fifty-eight days. You will join us, Lucia."

THAT NIGHT SHE SPOTTED ROSARIO AT the square moving in and out of circles like a mayor, as if he'd lived in San Salvatore all his life. He laughed easily and shook hands, clapped men on their backs. He bent low to talk to children, tickling them, pinching their noses.

Lucia chatted with her friends, casually tracking the movements of both Rosario and her father, who gestured wildly at the far end of the square, probably complaining about the drought. When Father Guilliardo stepped to the middle of the cobblestone road, followed by two altar boys and a deacon holding the St. Francis effigy, the townspeople closed in around him for the blessing. Deferentially, his hands behind his back, Rosario remained on the periphery, meandering around the circle.

As he neared her, Lucia sidled away from her friends and inched back. She stood on her toes and craned her neck to make it appear that she wanted a better look, then glanced to her left at the right moment. When their eyes met, they acknowledged each other with raised brows, Lucia grinning, conceding that she'd been caught at the very site she'd ridiculed, Rosario nodding and admonishing her like an old friend who knew she would be there.

He moved next to her. "We damn ourselves," he whispered.

"Shh."

Father Guilliardo held the aspergillum high and sprinkled holy water on St. Francis.

"So the Father wastes precious water?" he said.

"Shh." She pulled him by the shirt away from the others. "They will hear you."

He placed his hand over his mouth and glanced around furtively.

"You mock me," she said, half angrily. "You do not even know my name."

He stepped back and with his right hand lightly touching his chest, half bowed. "I am Rosario Antonelli."

"You mock me still," she said, but this time had to turn to hide her grin. She told him her name.

"Tell me, Lucia Tegolari, how old are you?"

"Seventeen."

He looked out past the square to the east, taking in the vast ridge of mountains that flanked the village. "Do you wish sometimes that you were older?"

"Seventeen is a good age, I think. Why do you ask?"

"I was merely thinking back." He pushed his hands in his pockets and sighed. "I couldn't wait to leave these landlocked fields."

Father Guilliardo cut the air with his pale hands, carving out the sign of the cross. He chanted a litany in Latin.

"Why did you return?"

He tugged at the kerchief around his neck, tightening it. "I did not like what I'd become."

"The university spoiled you."

The vagueness left his eyes and he smiled. "You are older than seventeen, I think."

It became clear to Lucia that no woman, certainly no girl, had ever talked to him this way, and that he enjoyed it. "And you are a boy."

"A boy?"

"You still do not know what you want."

"I want to breathe in. And I want to breathe out."

"You can do that anywhere."

"But you can't—"

"Shh." She pulled on his arm.

"But you can't. Don't you see? The city suffocates you. I mean this literally. Two factories with giant smokestacks opened within kilometers of the university. You get used to coughing and you barely notice, but I did not want to get used to it."

"You would rather get used to driving a mule around hillsides delivering what will someday spill from the sky and fill wells—and then what?"

Rosario turned and suppressed a laugh. "You do not ease up, do you?"

Lucia gazed at the dirt at her feet, hoping to appear more demure.

"So my task is not noble?" he said, still amused.

"I did not say that." She felt heat rise up in her.

"I provide sustenance."

Father Guilliardo completed his blessing and kissed St. Francis's feet.

Rosario stepped closer to Lucia and gripped her elbow. "I sustain," he whispered. "Don't you see?"

"And when it rains?"

"I breathe in. And I breathe out."

She backed away. "I breathe in, I breathe out. I breathe in, I breathe out. That is not an answer."

Like a wave, the crowd began to fall in around the center of the square for the procession through the northernmost fields.

"I must join my father," she said.

"Yes," he said. "I know."

She turned away.

"Lucia . . . have you ever been to the opera?"

Every Sunday morning a bus passed through San Salvatore and Faicchio and other villages to carry passengers to the rail station in Caserta. On the third Sunday following their meeting at the square, Lucia and Rosario boarded the bus at separate stops, sat apart, and gazed out their windows. Since her father usually spent all of Sunday playing cards at the bar, she didn't mention a word to him. And if anyone spotted her on the bus, they would most likely assume she was visiting her aunt and pay no mind. When the bus arrived at the rail station, they unloaded and waited at opposite ends of the wooden platform. It wasn't until they reached Naples, while walking to the opera house, that they spoke to one another.

"I'm not sure I like this secrecy," he said.

She stopped and let her jaw drop. "Rosario! It's so good to see you," she said. "What are you doing in Naples? I am on my way to the opera. Would you care to join me?"

He shook his head and sighed. "I suppose," he said wearily. "I have some friends, old classmates, who work at the San Carlo. Who might arrange to get us in."

"How fortunate."

They walked a while then, without speaking, Lucia taking in the symmetry of the city. Brick buildings squared off at rooftops. Narrow, inclined lanes lined for kilometers with three- and four-story flats on either side. Steel signposts. Yet the symmetry only highlighted the disorder. Labyrinthine clotheslines spread from sill to sill, the day's wash flapping like flags. Streets teeming with old men and women squabbling with vendors at corner markets. Months later when she tried to recall the day, this busyness was what she remembered.

Before they arrived at the San Carlo, Rosario guided her through the Santa Lucia district, pointing out the church of San Francesco di Paola, opened in 1817, and the Palazzo Reale that displayed in marble the various kings who ruled Naples, and the five-towered Castel Nuovo. Awestricken, Lucia tried to take in what she could, but she was more moved by Rosario's love of the city rather than by the city itself, and his love saddened her.

The opera, *La Bohème,* was a blaze of colors, a single breath, one sustained vibrato, background to what really mattered: sitting side by side in the dark, fingers clasped, not knowing or caring whether it was light or dark outside. When it ended, they walked back to the rail station, the sun high in the cloudless sky. Lucia clutched his hand, her eyes downcast.

"You did not enjoy it?" he said.

"No, no. It was wonderful."

"Then?"

For the first time that day she felt the dread of returning home, the fear of being caught, and she resented her father for piercing the opera dark stillness of her mind. Though she was willing to secretly violate her father's wishes, which would have forbid a trip to Naples with a man, she was not ready to confront him. She wasn't sure she ever would be. And it struck her suddenly that she had come to Naples so she *would* be caught. She wanted her hand forced. All she knew were drastic actions since this was all her father understood.

"Why did she have to die at the end?" she said.

"She had been sick."

"So why not a miracle?"

"You expected a miracle?"

"No, I knew she would die."

"Then?"

"I can hope, can't I? I can hope for a happy ending. No?"

She turned suddenly and kissed him on the mouth, and before he could respond, she pulled him by the hand toward the station.

THE NEXT FEW WEEKS BROUGHT NO relief from the drought, and Rosario continued his deliveries. Lucia would accompany him to the bell tower, where they would embrace and become as passionate as the cramped space would allow. Afterward, they would arrange to meet near the square where they would walk and gaze at the stars and not allow even their hands to touch until they were out of sight, behind a thicket. After weeks of seeing them together, the villagers must have surmised an affair of some sort, but Lucia didn't care. She knew they were less willing to confront her father than she was.

"I can see it in your eyes," she said one night.

"What?" he said.

"These hills will not keep you. There is little here to keep you."

They walked a little farther and when they reached a bench, Rosario sat and pulled her next to him. He ran a hand through his hair, ruffling it. Somewhere above them a mountain goat bleated stupidly. Lucia turned and tried to locate the source, but heard only the pulsating drone of cicadas. She didn't want to feel anything, so she pictured the goat running off, stopping to chomp on grass and every so often glance up lazily at the moon.

"What do I do when the rains come?" he said. "You asked that yourself, Lucia."

She wrung her fingers. "Yes, what do we do?" She nodded and her eyes glazed over as she stared at the clay at her feet. "When it rains." From the beginning she knew this moment would come. Come and pass, she thought. But she was surprised that she didn't feel anger at least. She was surprised he hadn't slipped away without notice and she wished he had.

"One of my professors. He wrote. About a job in Rome."

The words were a struggle for him, and she wanted to comfort him, make it easier for him, but she felt numb. She pictured herself pleading with him to take her along, but dismissed the image. He was not ready. And it would only drive him away sooner.

"When?" she said.

He wasn't sure, but when he didn't arrive the next week, she knew she would never see him again. If she acted more sullen than usual, her father didn't detect it, nor did any of her friends.

Less than a month after Rosario left, her father announced that he'd found a suitor for Lucia. They would be married, he said, within the year. When she heard, Lucia rose quietly from her chair and slipped into the kitchen. She started a fire under the stove and peeled potatoes. As they boiled, she scoured the floor and scrubbed the walls, wondering how she might have responded to her father's news if Rosario had not left. Would she have protested bitterly, then finally given in? Or would she have eloped? There seemed no other choice. But Rosario would not have agreed to escaping. He would have slipped away still.

This thought comforted her the rest of the evening, and she took it to bed, where she slept soundly, finally, until in the middle of the night the rumble of thunder awoke her. She sat up and pulled the sheet around her, pressing her lips to a fold in it, rocking. She remembered her mother sitting with her during nights like these, and though she wasn't afraid now, she longed for arms to cradle her. Single drops fell on the roof with a splat. She rose and walked to the door and opened it. A thin crescent moon poked through an opening in the clouds, illuminating the furrowed fields before her, and then it was gone. She stepped out into the inky darkness and let the drops fleck her cheeks. A crack of thunder startled her, but rather than retreating, she stepped out into the blackness. She closed her eyes and imagined the rain coming down now in long, silver pins. The rain streaked her eyes and mingled with the salty warmth there, and for a moment, a moment she hadn't allowed herself since he'd left, she was back with Rosario near the square, squeezing his hand, believing that his *aqua virgo* would sustain her.

In Motion

GIACOMO

C ANDICE'S MOM OPENED WIDE HER FRONT door and looked out
through the dirty screen. I peered in, trying to make out a face
in the silhouette but could find only two dull glares.

"Hi, my name is Jim Cummings," I said to the screen. "I'm the
one visiting with all the families with school-aged children. You're
Candice's mom, aren't you?"

Before she could answer, I blurted, "Fine," and reached down for
my sample case, leaned forward as I came up, and gripped the handle
of the screen. "May I come in?" I said, and strolled past her, listening
to the wood frame screen door bang shut loosely behind me.

It was that simple. After eight weeks, the word-for-word approach
and the broad smile got me into nearly every house—the nice white
bungalow with the sprawling willow that blotted out everything
but the corners of the house; the shack with the sagging porch and
the old rocker where Ma and Pa sat anyway and you didn't need
an approach; even the red brick fortress with its goddamn concrete

circular drive and manicured lawn. Candice's mom's house didn't have a circular drive or even a willow in front, but the porch wasn't sagging yet, either.

I glanced around, deciding how much time I could afford. On one wall hung a huge white starburst clock with brass numbers and brass trim. On another wall, hanging above the low droning television, was a painting of a gleaming black locomotive shooting through a pastoral green, white smoke billowing out the stack. The other walls were bare except for scattered purple and red crayon scribblings that seemed permanent. On the floor between a sofa and chair lay a crumpled white satin blouse with a green lollipop stuck to it. In front of the sofa was a glass table cluttered with paperbacks and coffee cups and a glass ashtray piled high with brown butts. Shit, if she had cash for cigarettes and lollipops, she had cash for my books. But I had to qualify her, make sure she could deliver today.

"People sure are friendly round here," I said with my eight-week-old Southern drawl. "It must be somethin' in the water ya'll drink." I started for the sofa. "Mind if I sit here?"

I didn't wait for an answer. It was a simple matter of motion. If you leaned forward and asked a question, the customer leaned forward. If you handed over the order book and casually let the pen roll to the floor, the customer reached for the pen, ready to sign. If you stood up, after slipping the check in your pocket, the customer stood.

I sank down on the sofa, while Candice's mom plopped down on the chair.

"Let me ask you a question," I said. "I need to get—"

"Say, where you from anyway, Jim?"

I was surprised she remembered my name. "Chicago," I said. "Like I was saying, I need to get—"

"How long you been in Oklahoma?"

"Oh, about three months." I fished through my sample case for an order book. "I need—"

"A boy come through here last summer too. Said he was from New York, working his way through college. You go to school up in Chicago?"

"Loyola," I said absently, reaching for my samples.

"So you'll be going back to school soon?"

"In about three weeks."

"How old are you?" she asked.

"Twenty," I lied. I figured *twenty* sounded more businesslike than eighteen.

I looked up. She wasn't much older than twenty herself and she certainly didn't look like a mother. She'd probably gotten pregnant and married at sixteen, had lived in a trailer home for a few years, worked as a waitress at night while her husband watched the baby, together had saved enough for a five percent down payment on the house, and now she was tired.

She sat back, her legs folded beneath her, her long fingers tapping on the shiny arms of the chair. The tapping seemed deliberate, as if she were deciding whether to light a cigarette. That would be natural: with the cigarette hanging loosely out the side of her mouth, she would shake that dark hair back, squint fiercely as she lit the cigarette, and then with only a slight turn, blow the smoke casually over her shoulder. But she didn't light one. She kept tapping.

She didn't have the kind of face you look at in awe, but she had a full mouth and the kind of fleshy lips that most guys like, which curled slightly open, as if always on the verge of muttering something. Her dull brown eyes were drawn and sunken as if from too many midnight shifts—or at least seemed sunken as they looked out through strands of long straight hair that hid most of her face. The hair was as coal black as mine, and I thought, she could have been my sister.

The fingers stopped, and she leaned forward. "Are you staying around here?" she asked.

Perfect. I explained that I was staying in Stillwater, which was about an hour away. With a start, I pointed to my watch. "It's past five o'clock, and— I need to get to a regular bank today. Do you do your banking around here?" I asked.

She did and she had a checking account. That's all I needed to know. I dug out the rest of my samples and looked for a spot to display them. Grabbing her paperbacks, I started to set them on the floor. "Do you mind if I move these?" I asked, knowing the answer.

She stood up. "No, not at all. You spread those books out real nice and I'll be right back. There's something I need to check on." She disappeared around the corner.

I cleared the table and carefully arranged my samples, the rainbow-colored children's books on the left, the large, glossy, red-and-white poster on the right. The poster had been folded and unfolded so many times that the creases were tearing. It had to last for my final three weeks though. There wasn't time to order a new one from the company, and without this one it would be nearly impossible to sell any package deals.

The packages would save me, I figured. I was doing okay, but I had told my brother, Michael, that I would come home at the end of the summer with three thousand dollars saved. He said I had gone off the deep end for taking a job with no salary. I showed him the books, explained about the fifty percent commission on every sale, how I'd have to make only three sales a day.

He shook his head the way big brothers do. Then he stood close to me, nose to nose, and started slapping my shoulders, pushing me around the kitchen. I kept backing up, asking him what the hell he thought he was doing. He said, "This is what you gotta be if you want to sell anything. Goddamn pushy." When he shoved me as far as I could go, I pushed him back, but he barely budged, which made him laugh.

He didn't understand. He hadn't been to the interview for the job or to sales school. He didn't know what it felt like to drive into a strange town, walk into a strange house, and walk out twenty minutes later with fifty dollars in his pocket. He didn't understand how it all had to do with motion.

The company understood. Which is why they insisted I move a thousand miles from home for the summer. That way I wouldn't have much choice other than to sell. Company's pushing you around already, Michael said.

Every Sunday when I phoned Mr. Herley in Nashville to review the week, I managed to kid him about the Great Movement Principle of the Universe, as we came to call it. One time I even abruptly hung up on him without warning. When he called back, I told him I knew he'd call. He understood immediately, and we both had a good laugh over it. Michael could never appreciate any of this.

I extended my arm to where Candice's mom had disappeared and tapped on my watch, as if this would get her back in the room. I didn't have time to sit around. I stood up and paced, jingling the keys and the coins in my pockets. I pulled out my ringed notebook and flipped through it, counting. Only thirteen demonstrations today. No wonder I didn't have any sales. I would have to move faster—work till nine thirty—whatever it took. I'd show Michael.

Where in hell was she?

I sat down and tapped my watch again, half-expecting that it would work, more than half-surprised when it seemed to. Above the hum of the TV I heard a door ease shut and an approaching pair of bare feet padding softly on the hardwood floor. I looked at the edge of the carpet, where it gave way to the scuffed floor, and waited for the feet. When they appeared, smooth and brown, I marveled at how the cute toes bunched together and bent easily with each step, at how the feet, instead of turning slightly left toward the chair, came directly toward the sofa. My eyes slid upward. Her long smooth legs seemed like they would never end, and even when they did they didn't. The washed-out denim shorts with the threads hanging ca- sually around the bottoms were tight enough to make out the very tops of the legs where they would be a vanilla white. She had on a plain white waitress blouse tucked neatly into her shorts, tucked to reveal that there was all skin beneath that crisp whiteness. Had she changed? My mind raced for a picture, but I couldn't remember—just the hair, and that was different. It was pulled back into a simple ponytail, which made her neck longer and her face, with its ruddy cheeks, younger. I looked at the eyes. They were still tired but they danced a little with the last rays of sun sifting through the window behind me.

She sat down on my left. I had the crazy impulse to shove my samples away and lunge out the door. I was wasting time. There was no sale here. Instead, I pointed casually to the three-in-one photo frame on top of the television. "That must be Candice there," I said.

"That was two years ago—on her first day of school."

Little Candice had on a green plaid jumper. She gripped a red pencil case in one hand and a lunchbox in the other. On her left, in the next frame, was a portrait of her mother with her hair piled high on her head; otherwise, she looked the same. On Candice's right was a portrait of a smiling young man in a military uniform.

"And is that your husband?" I glanced at her tight ponytail.

"Yes, that was him."

"Oh, I'm sorry. I just—"

"That picture was taken about three years ago, before the accident."

My stomach tightened a little. "That must really be rough for you and Candice."

"Well it's not too bad. We get a check every month."

I looked at her eyes to see if everything was all right. She was staring at the books on the table. Relieved, I picked up a book and shifted into drive.

"With Candice going into third grade, I think this first set, Young People's Adventure Library, would be especially helpful." I began to relax. I flipped open the book to the illustrated table of contents, turned toward her, held the bottom of the book deftly in one hand, and with the other, pointed out the different sections—which were now upside down to me.

I nodded and asked, "Can you see how this section on the presidents could help Candice in school?"

She slid closer and nodded.

"And can you see how this section on battles might make it easier to remember those dates?"

She nodded again. I decided to give her one of my abridged demonstrations and flipped through the pages to impress her with the colors of the flags and the battle scenes and the uniforms. I put the book down and pulled the large red-and-white poster to the middle of the table.

"You sure do have nice hair, Jim."

"Tha—"

"You must be I-talian."

"Well, yeah," I said weakly, gazing at the poster.

"There aren't too many I-talians around here. Least I don't know any. I thought all I-talian names ended with o."

"Well, my mother shortened the family name when she came over from Italy. It's really Comingo." I glanced at her. "You look like you could be Italian, too," I said blankly. I turned to the poster. Before she could break in, I said, "This next set covers basically the same material but in more depth." I waved my hand slowly across the ten history volumes on the huge poster so she could take in all the titles. "So you see, each volume becomes progressively more difficult. But Candice could still refer back to the previous volumes if she didn't understand something," I said, leaning over the poster.

She slid closer and leaned forward to look at the tenth volume. "Those sure are good books," she said.

"What I'm doing," I recited weakly, "is taking orders today and . . ." I droned on, suffocating.

With her hand on my knee, she leaned closer to look at that damn tenth volume, her back arched, her breasts pushing firmly against my shoulder where I could feel their soft roundness. I gripped the end of the table.

Without warning, she thrust her entire body forward and drove me to the floor in a crash. I was jarred, stunned. I looked up. Suddenly, she was all whispers and silky hair and warm flesh.

I found my breath and said, "Candice."

"Not home," she whispered absently.

I was about to say *husband* but remembered.

With a sigh, I rested my head on the floor, looked up at the ceiling as she kissed my face.

I worked my thumbs beneath her blouse and pulled it loose so my hands could slide freely along her curved back. My hands moved in a slow, circular motion, and I kept widening the circle until they came around to the sides and then, pushing her away a little to squeeze them in, to the front. I unbuttoned her blouse, peeled it off her arched shoulders. Still on top of me she managed to strip off my T-shirt, rubbed her chest on mine while her mouth worked on my neck. Her hands slid down to my thighs. I closed my eyes and drew in a deep breath. She let herself fall off to my side so she could work on the zipper, and she clutched it. Suddenly I heard something. She clutched at the zipper, but it wouldn't move. I heard something again, and my spine stiffened. I stared hard at the TV. She worked desperately, finally got the zipper to move, and stripped my pants down to my ankles. I heard it again. It wasn't the TV. I felt the cold clamminess of the poster under my back, felt it peeling away as I arched my head to listen. It whirred closer. My heart raced but I couldn't move. It got still closer, and all I could do was gaze at the spot where the carpet gave way to the scuffed hardwood and wait as the whirring became a loud groan.

A huge pair of burly feet appeared from around the corner. I bolted upright into a sitting position, my muscles rigid, blood rushing up my locked spine. The burly feet remained curiously still, resting on metal. They turned slightly and stopped.

I looked up and felt a pounding on my temples. He turned his head and looked down from his wheelchair. I stole a glance at the portrait on the TV and looked back. Our eyes became fixed.

It was like the first time the cops caught me with firecrackers and I knew I was cornered. I opened my mouth, but nothing came out. As if by instinct, he opened his mouth, but closed it again. His face was puffy and white. He scanned the area within his grasp, as if he were looking for something to throw, but I could see that he wouldn't be reaching or grabbing or hurling anything. He touched a lever on his armrest with the only finger that seemed able to, and the wheelchair lurched into reverse and disappeared. "Your hell is coming," he muttered. At least that's what I thought he said, like he felt sorry for us.

I looked down numbly, in a fog. Candice's mom lay there, resting her head on the poster, her eyes a glassy stare. Through the fog, it seemed like her head had become eerily superimposed onto the poster, two-dimensional. One hand still rested on my leg, the fingers lightly pawing, and I brushed them off.

My hands and feet moved as if I were trapped in a revolving door—trying to retrieve a shirt from one section, untangle pants in another, find change that had fallen from the pockets. Books tumbled. The door spun faster. I couldn't leave without the books.

I got outside, leaned against the side of my car, sample case in one hand, poster in the other. I gazed across the tarnished roof to the other side of the road, catching my breath. A gray-haired couple, holding hands, sat motionless on a porch swing. Beyond them, above the still leaves, the sky burned and cast long summer shadows. I looked down. I had crumpled the poster into a ball, and now it slipped to the ground, rolling beneath the car. I pictured Michael, felt his hands pushing me away. I wondered how I'd avoid telling him that maybe he was right.

I got in. Above the steering wheel, the gearbox letters seemed to pulse larger with each breath. I slammed the car into reverse and pulled out of the driveway, the tires crunching on the pea gravel, then drove away quietly down the hard black asphalt. The road wound around into another hollow full of dirt roads and dead ends. I drove faster, looking for a main highway, a paved road. I thought about being shoved to the floor, shoved hard, the way Michael had shoved me. She and I were alike, he'd say. She and I were alike. The car's rocking motion loosened the knot in my stomach and threatened to push everything up. When I finally found a road, I stopped, looked ahead at Candice's mom's house, and realized I was where I'd been.

On Hold

GIACOMO

THE SURGEON WARNED ME I'D GO stir crazy after a few weeks with the cast on and my leg elevated, but he didn't know Mama. He didn't know that I'd been leasing the top floor of a three-story brownstone with my buddy Ray, who I couldn't imagine waiting on me, and for those reasons would have to move back home for a few weeks. Reaching crazy wouldn't take but a few days.

I've often wondered how I'd deal with a physical impairment— paralysis, blindness, nothing so ordinary as a fractured tibia and fibula in my right leg—but I always imagined myself coping nobly, joking at the right moment so that a visitor felt at ease and maybe in awe of my spirit. Though I'd never factored in Mama.

I knew she'd be hysterical so I didn't even call her until Dr. Faddyun had inserted the rod that ran along the length of the tibia, the rod secured with titanium screws around the knee and the ankle. In fact, when the anesthesia wore off and I discovered that the cast covered every incision, I called and told Mama, simply, that I'd broken my leg, a small break, nothing serious, it would take a little time, that's all, and—I had to take a breath 'cause I couldn't believe what I was about to ask—would it be okay if I stayed with her and Papa for two or three weeks.

Would it be okay, she laughed, though she could not conceal her snideness. Would it be okay? A broken leg was my punishment, she probably thought, for moving out in the first place. "You stay two, three year," she said. "Why you give money to apart-a-ment?"

"Yeah, yeah, I know," I said. I was twenty-two years old was one reason. I moved out when I was twenty, a full two years after I'd spotted Mama in Connie's with a man other than Papa, an image that still seemed unreal to me, the same way that the death of a good friend seems unreal. And who could I tell? Who would believe it— Mama in a restaurant? With some man?

The urge to scream or throw something from her couch, maybe not directly at Mama but near enough, didn't arise until the pain subsided some and the phone stopped ringing and visitors trickled down to a few of Mama's friends who prayed over me like grieving crows. I wasn't very hungry that first or second day, so Mama took to wearing a black skirt with sheer black nylons and black slip-on shoes, the same outfit she'd wear for months after family funerals, except now she donned a starched white blouse instead of the usual black with the embroidered rosary on the pockets. There was still hope for me.

"Why you no eat?" she wanted to know.

I nearly let on and said, "I think it's the anesth—"

"Che?"

"The medicine they gave me for the pain. I don't feel too hungry."

"You eat, you make better."

"Yeah, Mama. That's what the doctor said, too. He said, You know, Jim, maybe we shouldn't put a cast on that leg. Maybe we should just cart you to the kitchen and feed you a bowl of pasta every hour. That's what he said, Mama. Maybe you should get a job there at the hospital."

But midway she had already dismissed me with a wave and gone off to the kitchen to chop vegetables for minestrone soup and to concoct yet another batch of marrow-mending chamomile tea spiked with some secret potion or other. I couldn't stomach even the scent from the steam, but I couldn't appease her without at least a sip or two. I swear there was some olive oil in that cup, her all-purpose elixir, along with maybe a shot of bourbon.

She'd apparently decided that she wasn't going to leave the house and had my brother, Michael, drop off groceries every few days, even though he lived more than fifteen miles away. Because of that, and because he was newly married, he never stayed long, but I welcomed the visit. We spent most of our time ribbing Mama the way we used to do. Papa, my other diversion, came home for lunch most days and after work sat with me for an hour or so, but then he was off to the park for boccie and his Marlboros. These were June nights and he needed to get out, too.

"You want I bring you something?" he asked each time, though he'd never driven a car in his life.

Yeah, Papa, I said to myself, bring back some gravel from the boccie pit. "No, Papa. You go. Have a good time." I wanted to add that maybe he shouldn't smoke too many at the park, but I didn't want to risk sounding like his wife.

As soon as I thought I could climb the stairs to my apartment without too much huffing and puffing, I'd take off, I reasoned. Two weeks maybe. Three weeks tops. But being back in that house wiped away all sense of consolation. I was thirteen again.

Part of that sinking feeling I attributed to the painkillers. Every time I shut my eyes I imagined myself scaling appliances or negotiating stairs before tumbling wildly, my arms flailing, and I'd have to open my eyes and grip the cushions of the couch to stop the reeling. Or I'd replay the fall, see myself behind the steering wheel and sliding the lever into park like I'd done a hundred other mornings, grabbing the *Sun-Times* bundle from the bay floor of the truck, readying myself for the leap onto the asphalt, one fluid motion, until the split sole of my right boot caught on the metal cleat that held down the brittle rubber flooring and that morning held my sole well enough to lock it in place while the rest of me soared forward, and before I touched ground I heard the snap, like the clean snap of a dry twig, nothing spectacular, but then the searing pain, and I became fluid again, resigned now for the inevitable thud and collapsed into myself, white heat flashing through my leg, my leg feeling separate now from my body, plummeting still, the news bundle finally cushioning my fall and saving my shoulder. And then I lay there for a while like it wasn't me, like somebody ought to come and help this poor guy.

Unconcerned with details, Mama never even asked how I'd broken my leg. She knew I was back home on her living room couch, and that was all she needed to know.

"You want I make chicka soup?" she asked.

"What, Mama?"

It was day six. I could sit up for thirty-minute stretches now without feeling too woozy, without a flash of fever slapping me prone again.

"Chicka soup," she repeated.

"It's eighty degrees out, Mama."

"I put a little noodle."

"I don't—"

"I no take long."

And she was off again, rattling pots, running water, chopping carrots. I sank down and fanned myself with a get-well card, my forehead burning. Apparently she spotted me and glided back to the couch to feel my head. She lamented to some saint or other and from the closet near the front door produced an oscillating fan, which she plugged in and set on the coffee table in front of me, not too close, of course, since swirling air might cause some mysterious ailment. Forget about the last fifty years of research on viruses.

"Thanks, Mama," I said.

I eyed a *Life* at the far end of the coffee table, wondering how to expend the least energy retrieving it. I wanted to finish an article on the UN, who reportedly paid soldiers $18,000 for a lost leg during peacekeeping operations; the article listed sums for other lost limbs too, and I wanted to compare. Mama saw and pushed the magazine toward me. She snatched two of the dozen pillows that surrounded the couch and propped up my head.

"What else you need?" she asked.

I'm sure you'll tell me, Mama. Just a little air maybe. Not fan air. Air that hadn't been swallowed by this fishbowl of a house, a squat bungalow with three small bedrooms off the narrow living room and dining room that led to an even narrower kitchen. With two healthy legs you could walk a straight line from the couch to the kitchen sink. There was no place to hide.

On day ten Mama gave me a St. Christopher's medal and had Father Joe from St. Columbkille in the old neighborhood pay me a visit, the same Father Joe whose confessional I'd peed in when I was eight or nine because *I couldn't hold it.* Peed in my pants actually, the warmth trickling down my legs and, though I was kneeling, into my socks. I strained to create a space between my skin and pants but soon felt the blotting and the sticking and kept pulling the material away, the sharp yellow smell pushing through the muskiness of the dark booth. When Father Joe slid open his paneled window, and all that separated us was latticework and a black scrim curtain, I wondered if I'd sinned and if I should report the deed. I didn't, of course, and after I'd been assigned my three Hail Marys and three Our Fathers for lying to my parents or some such other serviceable sin, I ran home without turning back.

Sitting across from me now in Mama's living room, Father Joe had a broad, fleshy face and the pasty complexion of a corpse who'd been made up with the chalky paint of a funeral parlor. Though I didn't believe him, he said he remembered me serving mass for him.

"Some memory, Father," I said. "I really enjoyed those days." The bittersweet incense that burned into the layered coats of varnish on the mahogany pews. The smoke that rose in gray-white clouds from the incense kettle. The brass Eucharistic bells, rung twice on cue, though I could no longer recall the telltale words. The chink of the wineglass against the chalice. Small moments that kept my breath suspended.

He crossed his legs, leaned back, and peered down at me. "I remember everything, Jimmy."

Even the rank puddles left in your confessional? I wanted to ask.

"Your mother is taking good care of you, I trust."

After setting down sweets, espresso, and a bowl of fruit on the coffee table, Mama demurely slipped out to the backyard, in case I wanted to confess and purge myself of the sin that had fractured my tibia.

I glanced at the table. "Well, when I first came home out of the hospital, I wasn't hungry much." I patted my belly. "But I've gained a few since then."

He chuckled politely and went on about how when I felt better I'd need to exercise. Then he got this faraway look in his eyes, as if he just drudged up some sermon he'd given on prayer being the exercise for the soul, and reminded me of the power of prayer. I tried listening—I really did—he had a kind voice and I wanted to apologize for soaking his confessional, but my energy soon waned as it usually did during lofty sermonizing, and my thoughts drifted—if a deaf man falls in the forest and breaks his leg, will his screams make a sound?—so I turned to the window and adopted my most pensive lockjaw gaze.

Looking out, I remembered running, blazing up and down streets like these on summer nights on two solid legs, pumping and gliding and wheezing. Not a worry to weigh me down. Not till I stopped. Only then did I contemplate the catch in my breath, the searing ache deep in my throat, and wondered about the clock, worried that I'd stayed out too late and would have to suffer Mama's wrath. She should have understood. Stopping never agreed with either of us. We were always doing. Being laid up now, temporarily out of commission, on hold, I felt like a husk. Staring out that window, I decided we were all nothing more than husks. Words dribbled out of Father's mouth but they would sink into the carpet and he'd take his husk elsewhere and elsewhere until he could no longer command it, until it was no longer his, this shell, this second-rate rental that would fail him soon guaranteed. Not that this was any jolting revelation—I remember my abhorrence to communion back in eighth grade because the procession to the altar reminded me not *of the body of Christ* but that each of us was inching closer and closer to death—but I *felt* it now, deep in my bones, in my tibia, in my fibula, in every other bone I couldn't name, I felt it. I could have just as easily fractured both legs or my hip or my skull—there wasn't that much separating whether I breathed or not.

I turned and looked at Father's black shoes, dull but not a scuff on either of them.

"Father," I said.

He stopped.

I looked into his eyes, blue pools of reassurance.

"Would you, would it be okay if I made confession, if I confessed?"

Without a word he brought his chair closer to the couch, sat facing the living room picture window, and bowed his head. He crossed himself, a string of incantations spilling threadlike from his lips, and he was ready.

I needed more dark. The afternoon sun poured through the window in glimmering shafts of gold and even with my eyelids closed splintered through. "Bless me, Father," I said and made the sign of the cross, "for I have sinned. It has been . . . many years since my last confession. I've been . . ."

But I couldn't do it. I had the words all right, but the old knee-jerk reflexes kicked in and I heard myself spitting out the same third-grade sins the nuns had taught us to recite. The sisters had meant well to offer suggestions, but most of us simply memorized and juggled the list from week to week. Shame overtook me, not because *I had lied* and *been mean* to my parents and not because I *had impure thoughts*, but because I didn't have concrete, adult sins to report. Because I couldn't tell him about the time I saw Mama in a restaurant with another man and have acted since then more like a stranger than a son to her, a cruel and deliberate decision that pierces her like a dagger and that both pleases and kills me. Somewhere along the way I learned to live with my daggers. She deserved it, I figured. Look how she treats Papa. Besides, I reasoned, I'm no match for her. Nothing pierces her really. She puts others in their place and assumes control with the wave of her hand; she's able to shunt it. But I catch the hurt in the exasperated sighs that would give way to real sobs if she'd allow it. I catch the hurt in the flinching of her eyes as she turns away and in the blank stare as she gazes at a distant spot on the floor.

When it became clear that I'd exhausted my list, Father turned to bless me and moved his chair to its original position.

"No Hail Marys? Our Fathers?" I asked.

He seemed mostly relieved that I hadn't been more candid—after all, we were strangers, really, sitting in a bright, cramped room—but he also sensed my shame, I think.

"The church has changed some, Jimmy. I've changed. Some people find comfort in confession, and others need . . . something else. Would you—do you *need* me to assign penance?"

"I suppose the blessing is enough," I said. More than I deserved probably for my pathetic sins.

"Confession is about atonement, Jimmy. Reconciliation. How many Our Fathers will that take, son?"

After he left I fell asleep. And slept a good portion of the next day. The lying around and the extra weight around the middle and the heat were sapping me.

"Mama," I called. "Mama!"

Her head appeared outside the kitchen screen door from which I could actually feel a cutting breeze that evening.

"Che voglia?"

I rubbed my eyes and listened to the screen door slam and Mama's feet slap across the kitchen floor. The familiarity of those steps made my chest ache. "You know that book you have, Mama. The one with all the old pictures. Pictures from Italy. You know where that is?"

She disappeared into her bedroom and came back with a mud-colored scrapbook, a few corners of the plastic overlays poking out in dusty triangles. The gilt-rimmed edges of the ebony pages caused them to stick, so as I turned through the album I was greeted with a harsh creaking that seemed fitting. Most of the photographs had retained the sharp contrast of blacks and whites, but some of the oldest were washed in a rich sepia. Except for the photograph that I was after and miscellaneous others, the book was a collection of stiff-backed portraits of individuals, couples, and family groupings.

"Wait, Mama." She was already on her way out to the garden. "Come here."

She sat down on the same chair that Father Joe had occupied the day before, and I handed her the photo. In it, she is twelve or thirteen, sitting on the stoop of her farmhouse, her dark eyes lit with delight. Her hair is pulled back simply, her forehead lightly smudged, most likely from the back of her hand as she wiped away a ring of perspiration, a familiar gesture. She has been working in the fields, her fingers are soiled, the bottom of her dress, if it can be called that, is frayed. Yet she finds a moment to sit and laugh, and someone else finds a moment to snap the shot, one of the few candid photographs in the entire album.

"Do you remember when this was taken?"

She held the picture with the tips of her left index finger and thumb, and with her other hand tapped her knee.

"Long time ago," she said.

I looked out the window. Dusk was fast approaching. The lights at the park would be flickering on soon, and Papa would be hurling his boccie balls down a stone alley.

"You were happy then," I said.

Out of the corner of my eyes I could see her staring at her old self and nodding. "You like this pitch?" she said softly. "You keep."

I thought she might jump up from her chair and race out again, but she didn't move. She fingered the scalloped edges of the photograph with both hands, as if the picture had taken on new value now that it had been offered away.

"No, you should keep it, Mama. I was just wondering. I woke up and thought about that picture. What were you looking at that made you so happy?"

I was afraid she'd catch the insinuation: happy then, not now. But she seemed lost in the photograph.

"*Nonna,*" she said, nodding. "She make me laugh."

"Your mom?"

"*Si!* All the time she make me laugh."

It dawned on me that Nonna had died when Mama was thirteen,

which must have been shortly after the picture was taken. A lifetime ago. But the memory, it seemed, was as clear as the image in her hand.

"*La fotografía*. Why you rememb?" She smiled but couldn't conceal her sadness. She placed the photograph on the coffee table between us.

"I dreamed about it, I think." In the dream, I'm running. Moving through a green field, approaching the stoop, Mama sitting there, thirteen years old, grinning, glad to see me. "Do you wish you could go back?" I said.

"Someday I go."

"No, I mean a long time ago. Do you wish you could go back to that day in the picture?"

She gave me one of those looks that usually preceded *You crazy* or *Stupido* but she stopped herself. She laughed and said, "I dream, too, maybe. Tonight I go back."

We sat there a while longer, both of us gazing at the photograph of this thirteen-year-old girl who would know about death soon, and marriage and children, and infidelity too, and who would know about death again soon enough. But for the moment, a rare quiet moment the length of a breath maybe, with her son on the couch, helpless as a boy and vowing silently to forgive, the push of time seemed gently suspended.

Silences

Jim Cummings drove around in circles, the back of his neck burning, the throbbing in his head now slow and steady. It wasn't the beer, he knew. He wished to God it were. Hours earlier at his bachelor party, he had climbed onto a hooker. His skin crawled now at the thought of it. What had he been thinking? He spat out the window. Spat again. Suddenly two yellow beams of light washed over him, and in an instant swerved away. He pressed hard on the horn, the blare cutting through the August stillness. He cussed the bastard.

He pulled in front of his apartment, looked up at the darkened third-floor window. Six months before, he and his fiancée, Teri, and his best-man-to-be, Rick, had lugged furniture up the three flights of stairs. After Rick left, he and Teri had collapsed to the floor in exhaustion, rolled playfully on top of each other, excited and scared, and made love to each other for the first time. It had been Teri's first time ever.

How many other parties had the hooker worked tonight? he wondered. He started the car again and peeled it away from the curb, almost hitting the parked van in front of him. When he got to Teri's house, he didn't dare glance at her bedroom window and didn't slow the car. He drove a few more blocks to the church where they would be married, pulled into the lot, and parked. He stared blankly at the rectory where he and Teri had filled out forms at eight that evening, just seven hours ago. He hadn't been in a rectory since his altar boy days in eighth grade. Sitting close to Teri, waiting for Father Rourke, who would pronounce them married in two weeks, he had been struck by the old schoolboy emotions of awe and fear for the place.

He had leaned over and whispered, "What do you think he's going to ask us?"

She pushed him away playfully. "Why are you whispering?"

He laughed, a bit disappointed that she wasn't as awestruck with the rectory as he was.

She squeezed his hand. "Are you nervous?" she asked.

"A little."

"Relax. All he'll want to know is how many times you've disobeyed your parents in the past three months, how often you've lied to me, and how many people you've murdered."

He nodded knowingly. "Exactly."

They had both attended Catholic schools in the city, had recited the same confessions. He remembered the nuns, how they would wait outside the church confessionals and review beforehand the common sins on their checklists with each boy and girl.

Sometimes they would unsheath red pens from dark places beneath their habits, warning that what they wrote in their blue books would "go on your records forever." He imagined Father Rourke calling St. Columbkille, requesting the records. "So, James," he'd say. "About the time you demolished the milkman's truck, how many Our Fathers did you recite for that? Or what about that Halloween night when you broke the third-floor window with an egg—or the firecracker you blew off in school? How do you explain all this, my boy?"

His eyes slid up to the silver crucifix on the wall. The other records, the unwritten ones, would never fade, he knew. He *had* slept with three other girls, all during college, which he had confessed to Teri, who, as much as she tried to seem understanding, remained remote for a few days. And except for Christmas days and the few times that Teri had dragged him along, he hadn't been to church in over ten years. He prayed that neither of these things would disqualify him from being married in the Catholic church, worrying that Teri might not marry him if the church disapproved.

"If he asks, 'Are you Catholic?' 'what should I say?" asked Jim.

"Well, are you?"

He turned to her. She had honest, blue eyes, forgiving yet knowing. If it weren't for those eyes, thought Jim, and her straw-colored, schoolgirl curls, she would look pale and skinny, with her straight nose and long chin.

"I was baptized," said Jim. "I made my communion and confirmation." He was embarrassed to mention his living room confession with Father Joe. "But I haven't made a confession really since Sister Ernestine whacked me across the ass with a ruler in eighth grade."

"You probably shouldn't swear in a rectory," she teased.

"Since she whacked me across the rear end. And I hardly ever go to church. Don't you think all that will make a difference?"

"Just tell him how you feel. You're a good person."

He sighed and gazed at the ceiling. As a kid he had spent hours staring at the ceilings of St. Columbkille. I'm a good person, he told himself, with less conviction, he thought, than Teri had said it. He was trying. But the past had a way of creeping back. In college, he got by rewriting his friends' papers, taking the right teachers whose main requirements were attendance.

After college, he sold pharmaceuticals and medical supplies for small companies that paid him a draw against commission. The only way to make a salary was to sell. He worked steadily but never broke any records. After a while, he found himself lying more and more to create sales, and liking himself less. When he met Teri two years ago, she convinced him to get out of sales since it made him so miserable. She always had a way of making his problems seem simple and uncluttered.

She even seemed to understand his past and easily teased him about it. She had sent him a note one time using a mock letterhead from St. Columbkille Church. Father Jakiniewski, the new pastor, wanted Jim to make an appointment, the letter stated, to explain the shortage in altar boy cassocks. He had expressed his amazement to

Teri for days. How could they have tracked him down? He wasn't worried about the money or the consequences, but that they had found him. He looked at her with puzzled concern that one day in the park. Shafts of sunlight filtered through the leafy branches behind her. Her eyes sparkled. Her mouth became tightly pursed, holding back the laughter. She looked down and covered her face, her whole body shaking. Then he had chased her, at full speed at first, then slowing down. He wanted it to last, like a scene from some movie. It was while he chased her, listening to her wheezy laughter, that it first occurred to him that he wanted to marry her.

When he heard Father Rourke approaching, heels click-clacking and echoing against the tile floor, he thought he understood, for a moment, the awe he felt for the rectory. It was the deep silence of the place, a silence that had always seemed profound and magical to him as an altar boy, something about it that was always just out of reach of his understanding.

They both stood as Father Rourke strolled in.

"Hi, Father," said Teri. "This is Jim. Jim, this is Father Rourke."

They shook hands. "Oh, fine, fine. Have a seat, have a seat. Sorry to keep you waiting."

Jim nearly laughed aloud at his sharp Irish accent, his puffy red cheeks, the bulbous nose. His face was on fire.

"Ah, this is the most joyful part of my job." He beamed. He sifted through a drawer and pulled out several forms, slapping them on top of the desk. "Now, will you spell your full name . . . James, was it?" He wrote quickly, with long strokes, dotting every period with pro-

nounced flare. "Social security number? . . . Phone? . . . Catholic—"
He glanced up at Jim's dark Italian face. "Yes, of course. Practicing
Catholic? Yes." He quickly X'd both boxes. He paused and gazed
gravely at Jim, who promptly straightened and folded his hands.
"Jim," he said. "Have you ever committed a mortal sin?"

Jim felt a pounding in his ear. Did mortal sin mean premarital
sex? "I haven't murdered anyone," he said.

They all chuckled, Father Rourke laughing the loudest.

"A little clerical humor," he said, and scanned the rest of the form.
"I don't really need to know."

The meeting lasted only fifteen minutes. Outside the rectory,
Jim's steps were light. He felt like a boy dismissed early from school.
Teri lagged behind.

He turned. "What's wrong, honey?"

"Oh, it's nothing."

"What is it?"

She looked down. "I don't know. He's going to marry us in two
weeks and he hardly knows us."

He pulled her in tightly. "The important thing is that we
know each other . . . right?" He bent down to look straight in
her eyes.

"I know," she said.

He released her but kept hold of her hands. "You don't sound
very convincing," he said softly.

"No, you're right. It's just that . . . men don't understand,
that's all."

"Do you want to sit down and talk?"

"Tomorrow," she said. "I know you have to go. The boys are waiting."

"Are you sure? They can wait."

"I'm sure. Go ahead. Say hello to Rick."

They hugged good-bye and got into their cars. As they pulled away, they rolled their windows down and waved. "Be careful driving home," yelled Teri. "And behave."

Teri would be all right, he thought. She had spent hundreds of hours planning the wedding, and with only two weeks left, she was nervous. Even the best plans never worked out perfectly, Jim knew.

When he arrived at the apartment at eight thirty, Rick was there alone watching the first preseason football game, the Bears against the Cardinals.

"Hey, old man," said Rick. "Come on in." Rick wore a faded Bears T-shirt and Hawaiian shorts that showed his stick legs. He had always looked to Jim like a ferret.

"Where is everybody? Way to take care of me, Rick."

"I forgot about the game. I should have told everyone to come over to watch it." He sank into the couch. "It's a great game. The Bears are down three and they just recovered a fumble inside the twenty."

Jim scanned the apartment. Football had never interested him much. The only times he watched any games were when Rick had extra tickets, and even then he spent his time stopping Rick from jumping onto the field or assaulting another fan.

"You even cleaned up this sewer," said Jim. "I'm touched."

"Anything for my pal," said Rick, making a clicking sound out the side of his mouth like he always did.

"How much time?"

"Under three minutes." He crouched forward toward the TV. "Hey, grab a beer, will ya? This is your night. We're going to take care of you."

When the game ended thirty minutes later, one other person had arrived, a mutual friend of theirs whom Jim hadn't seen since college.

"A great game," said Rick. "Tomorrow I'm going downtown. Buying season tickets."

"I'll start saving bail money," said Jim.

"Right, old man. You're the one going to jail—in two weeks."

Jim pointed to the empty chairs. "Not if I don't have a bachelor party. Where the hell are these guys?"

"Game's over. They'll be here."

Jim wondered who would show up. Except for a few friends from work, most of his buddies were also Rick's friends. It seemed that when he met Rick in college, in a political science class, where Rick had casually mentioned using a term paper service, a new network of friends suddenly opened up to him. It amazed him how minor incidents, chance meetings, had a way of shaping people's lives.

By ten, the small apartment was filled. A small fan in the kitchen where the keg lay whirled out thick smoke, but did nothing for the sticky, August humidity. Someone opened the front door and several people drifted into the hallway. Sixties music blared from huge speakers in the living room where two people danced side by side mouthing lyrics into invisible microphones. Every few minutes someone patted Jim on the back or shook his hand and made sure that he had a beer.

After a while, and Jim would later try to recall the precise numbers on the digital clock atop the TV when it happened, the talking became distinctly hushed, almost quiet. Jim thought the beer had dulled his senses, or, looking around, that maybe the police had arrived. Everyone seemed to be stealing glances at him, snickering. Rick rushed through the apartment and out the door, as if late for an appointment. Moments later he returned, marched straight to Jim, and brought him to the center of the living room.

"Move that chair here," ordered Rick to no one in particular. He pushed Jim into the chair. Short of breath, Rick raced back to the door and motioned for someone to enter.

In strutted a lanky girl with long silvery hair, strawberry red lipstick, cheeks caked thick with rouge. A huge man with big boots followed, closing the door and leaning against it, waiting. The girl walked straight to Jim.

"I hear congratulations are in order, Jim." She shook his hand.

Everyone groaned in disapproval. "You can do better than that," someone shouted.

Jim put up his hands. "No, no, I'm a married man," he said

gravely, getting a laugh. His face flushed, he tried to push his chair out of the center, into the circle that had formed around him.

"Don't be shy," said the girl, as she pulled him back to the center, provoking a round of whooping and whistling.

Jim tried backing away again. "Guys . . . hey, you didn't have to do this. Really." He surveyed the room to find Rick, to whom everyone seemed to be slipping dollar bills. "Rick, help me out here," he pleaded.

"Someone get him a beer," bellowed Rick out the side of his mouth.

"Rick," said the girl. "How about some dancing music?" She sat Jim down.

"Sure, baby," answered Rick.

Someone pushed a beer into Jim's hands. A Motown tune suddenly blared. The girl started dancing, swirling her hips, prancing left and right in front of Jim.

Having resigned himself to the fact that he was part of the show, Jim sat back, let the girl take control, hooted and hollered with everyone else. He wondered how much she would take off, not particularly interested in seeing her naked. Besides, how excited could he get, he thought, with thirty guys watching.

She unbuttoned her blouse and let it brush by his face as she passed.

"Does your mother know you do this?" asked Jim drunkenly.

With a pasted smile, the girl kept moving.

Jim looked at the man with the boots, was about to say, Is

that your father? but didn't. He wasn't that stupid, he thought, or that drunk. Instead, he said, "We've got to stop meeting like this, honey."

She peeled off her blouse and rubbed her small breasts against his face, her pelvis rotating. She took his hands, one of them still holding the beer can, and let them run down her chest, the beer spilling onto her.

A bit aroused, Jim guzzled the rest of the beer. "Hey, my beer's warm all of a sudden. What's going on?" Everyone roared. When did he become so funny? he wondered.

Still dancing, she slid off her pants, tried to pull his head to her lower torso, but he resisted. "Whoa," he barked. "I don't stick my head between any girl's legs on the first date." He looked up at her face, wanted her to laugh, but got back just the pasted smile. It had become a bit thin and strained, Jim thought.

She circled behind him, clawed her fingers beneath his shirt, and ripped it open, the buttons flying to the grimy carpet.

"Rick . . . help me, Rick . . ."

"I thought I told you guys to get him a beer," yelled Rick.

Three beers were suddenly pushed at him. As he got up to grab them, all three of them for the laughs he knew would follow, the girl unloosed his pants and deftly pushed them down to his knees. When he sat to put the beers down, to free his hands, she yanked the pants from the bottom.

He sat there in the center of the living room wearing underwear and black socks, looking lost. "I tell you," he said, an edge of confidence gone now from his voice, "you'd better take some assertiveness training courses."

Rick weaved his way to the man with the boots, who counted the money and nodded to the girl.

"This one's a regular comedian," she said. "We've got ways of dealing with his kind." She grabbed Jim's hand and pulled him from his chair. She looked to Rick, who signaled a direction with his thumb. "Let's go," she said.

With everyone clearing the way in front and pushing from behind, Jim could hardly resist. He felt like a boy, his mother dragging him home for supper. "What the hell is going on . . . hey, Rick . . . Rick . . ."

She pulled him into the bedroom and shut the door. The room was a sauna. Sweat streamed down his face. It sobered him immediately. The girl lay on the bed, motioning him to her like some shoe salesman.

The last few moments had moved fast, he thought. He turned to the closed door. It would be easy to stand at the door for five minutes and walk out with a big smile. She had gotten paid; she wouldn't care. He turned to the girl, shook his head and snickered. When he was twelve he had dreamed of situations like this.

He searched for a towel to wipe his face and bent down to use the bedspread. His eyes slid up. She was still there, welcoming him. A wave of energy swept through him, his breath cut short for a moment.

What was stopping him? he asked himself. He wasn't married,

had made no official commitments yet. He deserved a reward now and then. Besides, this meant nothing. It was a matter of two membranes touching. In five minutes it would be over, and he wouldn't have to pretend how good it was to thirty guys in the living room. And what if they found out—

As he crawled on top of her, his thoughts raced back to the rectory. Even Father Rourke, holed up in that fortress, would understand. He probably had a form: "How many premarital encounters? Is it three or four? Three, four . . . doesn't make that much difference now, does it, Jim?"

When he was done—it had been like a quick visit to a grungy clinic—he marched to the kitchen in his underwear, grabbed two beers, and yelled to the living room for his pants. They flew across the apartment and landed at his feet. He drank one of the beers quickly, grabbed another, and wandered back to the living room. Rick winked at him, slapped him on the back: "I told you we'd take care of you." Jim nodded and held up his beer for a toast, acting drunker than he really was. He downed it quickly. With the other beer still in his hand, he yelled, "Get me a beer."

The numbers on the clock read 3:42 when he woke up. He couldn't remember when he had passed out. He searched around. The apartment was empty. He grabbed an open beer can and forced himself to swallow what was left. It was warm and salty, worse than the elixirs his mother had prepared for him as a boy. He downed the last few ounces of another can and left.

Sitting there in his car, a hundred feet from the spot where he would make his vows, he could still taste the cotton bitterness of the beer. He pulled out of the church lot and drove around for a long while before deciding to stop by the old neighborhood. It seemed somehow shrunken to him. He pulled up to St. Columbkille School, remembering all the games played there, games that held him fascinated as a boy: hide-and-seek, ring-a-levio, bluff poker. He was never good at the bluffing part. As desperately as he tried, he was never good at being one of the guys.

He got out and walked around the school to the attached church and tried one of the doors. Locked. He stepped back, peered up at the enormous facade with its stained-glass windows and grimy concrete swirlings. What did he do last night? he asked himself. He tried another door, then another. His neck burned. It hadn't cooled off at all during the night. He needed to find a priest, make a confession. He tried the final door—sometimes they left a single door unlocked, he remembered. He tugged hard, dropped down to his knees. He didn't need a priest, he decided. He could confess to God. "Bless me, Father— Bless me, God," he whispered, a tightness forming at the back of his throat. "It has been . . . three years since my last confession. During that time I have lied, I have sworn . . . Last night I—"

He stood. Why should God suddenly listen to him? he thought. He shuffled back to his car, kicking a small stone, watching it skid across the blacktop. His throat itched. He looked up at the stars and drew in stinging sighs.

Last night was an isolated lapse, he decided. It didn't erase the past two years, and it wasn't an indication of the future. Tomorrow, he would pick up Teri, take her to a movie. Afterward at dinner, they would discuss the wedding plans, iron out the remaining details. Then he'd drive her home, the radio humming softly, the same constellations burning in the sky, and only he would hear the silence between them.

City Hall

MICHELINO

Tʜᴀᴛ ᴛɪᴍᴇ Pᴀᴘᴀ ᴀɴᴅ I ᴡᴇɴᴛ down to Dearborn Street, down to city hall, you couldn't see three feet in front of you the snow was coming down so hard. It fell in stark white sheets, whipping around, slapping us in our faces. Papa wasn't one to complain, you see, but I expected him to tap me on the arm and suggest that we turn back to Union Station and forget the ten- or fifteen-block walk to Dearborn. I would've flagged down a taxi if he'd said something, but he trudged along, shoulder to shoulder with me. The only uncertainty I had was about which name I'd choose: Michelino Pietro Comingo or Michael Peter Comingo. Papa's choice was easy; he just had to reclaim Comingo. The name to me was full of character, robust and enduring—unlike Cummings, which even as a boy had seemed flimsy to me. I never understood Papa's meager response to my idea. Sure, he'd have to put up with Mama's cries about taking a day off from work for foolishness. But he was in his sixties and had been warding off her complaints for more than thirty years. I think he knew that no matter what he did, she'd still attack him. So that wasn't it. And I don't think he was worried about losing a workday. I'm not sure what it was. It seemed like reclaiming Comingo was just a gesture to him, like he was going along for my sake.

When the clerk with his crooked, maroon bow tie pushed the form in front of me, I remember feeling profound disappointment. The lines on the form were splotchy and faded from years of photocopying. The clerk peered over the rims of his bifocals beyond me to the waiting area full of foreigners, assessing, it seemed, how many people he'd have to process before he could take a break. His eyelids were heavy. He was beyond being annoyed.

I felt something like compassion for the foreigners behind me with their mismatched clothes and frightened looks. If Mama— and later Papa—hadn't immigrated thirty years ago, I would likely have been among them. But while they, I'm sure, were assuming shorter, American names—lopping off endings, discarding unnecessary vowels—Papa and I were extending our legacy, throwing out tug lines across the Atlantic, linking us with what I hoped was a long, rich tradition of Comingos. I intended to find out about those roots, intended to trek back to Italia one day, delve into my heritage, and I felt my new name, my birth name, would be the first step of the journey. Comingo was my passport.

Without thinking really, I picked up the pen, rolled it between my finger and thumb, and finally wrote, "Michelino . . . Pietro . . . Comingo."

The Casket

MICHELINO

I FIGURED HE'D KILLED HER. MY WIFE, Gale, told me to stop figuring and paint the bathroom. A bathroom painted or unpainted doesn't really matter in the long run. Gale prefers to fret about furry toilet-seat covers and print shower curtains. How do you argue with that? She'd end up pecking away at me like old Mrs. Weed next door does—or did—to her little husband. I didn't really believe he killed her, you see, but I hadn't seen either of them in weeks and I have to admit, when dusk closed in around their brick bungalow each night, I felt something prickly and cold up the back of my neck. He could have done it. I mean it does happen. Since we were new in the neighborhood, six months, it was natural to imagine.

I remember that first day. The We Move the Earth truck rattled away, and the Weeds pulled into their crumbling driveway at about the same time. I started over to meet them, while Gale and our daughter, Justy, got settled inside. Mrs. Weed, heavy-set, square-shouldered, marched toward me when she spotted me. Sliding off one shoulder was a faded-gray housedress, the kind that should be worn only inside the house. I mean, I didn't want to see her shoulders.

"Hi. I'm Michelino Comingo," I said. "Michael."

She ignored my outstretched hand and pointed to her husband. "This is Mr. Weed and I'm Mrs. Weed," she said, like I was a kid. I wanted to tell her I was thirty-eight, that my back went out about every few months, that I had to catch my breath sometimes just walking to the train station. I wanted to tell her that I was a father and that I made a decent living selling globes for Rand McNally.

But she didn't say *Weed*. It was *Leed* or *Leeb* or maybe even *Weeb*. I wanted to ask them to repeat it, but I was embarrassed for them, that they hadn't used their first names. Later, when I told Gale, I said "Weed" and the name stuck.

"Let me show you something," Mrs. Weed said. She turned and walked to the edge of my lawn, the boundary line between our properties. I followed her. She pointed to our backyards, her other hand resting on her hip. I think she might even have tapped her foot in annoyance.

"See that willow in your yard?" she said. "It's in my airspace. If one of those branches falls, it'll smash a goddamn hole in my garage roof." Her voice was loud and shrill, but matter-of-fact. This was how she talked to her neighbors, I figured, as if she were a weary umpire rattling off the ground rules.

I wanted to start on the right track, so I didn't argue. "Oh," I said, knowing she'd continue.

"Oh?" she said. "Gary lived here"—she glanced at her husband—

"what? Four, five years?" She turned to the tree again. "Never trimmed it once. Oh, I told him, all right. One night a storm blew a branch off, went right through my goddamn roof."

She spoke briskly, as if she'd been waiting months to tell me all this, probably ever since she saw the FOR SALE sign. The whole time she never looked at me, never looked, really, at her husband. He'd mumble or echo his wife: "Oh, yeah, willow needs trimming, all right," he'd say, and point a finger at it, ready to tell his own story about the willow, but she'd interrupt and leave him with his finger in the air and his mouth half-cocked.

As she went on about Gary's negligence, Mr. Weed shifted his weight from one foot to the other, his shoulders hunched, his back bent—probably from years of shifting and waiting—and ran a hand through his stark white hair. It was short and wiry, like a scouring pad. When his wife paused, he tapped me on the arm. "Eighty-one years old," he said. "Still got all my hair. The gray don't bother me none. Least it's all there." He nodded and gazed up at me from his crooked stance, his face blotted with raw, red blotches.

Then Mrs. Weed started up again. In mid-sentence, without pausing, she pointed behind her to something next to their fifteen-foot evergreen tree in front. The tree was dying and I thought, How do you kill an evergreen? The old man turned and hobbled to the tree and picked up this thing—Gale and I later named it his casket, *il cofanetto;* well, I did actually, but she went along—and he placed the thing at the entrance to their driveway.

"Garbage pickup tomorrow?" I asked Mrs. Weed.

"No. Thursday," she said and continued her litany.

It was some kind of makeshift wheelbarrow, a metal box really, rusted and dented, scratched patches of red paint still visible. It lay upside down, a single wheel bolted to the bottom. Mr. Weed spun the wheel once with the tip of his index finger and grinned, then returned to his wife.

"Made that myself," he said.

"Made what?" said Mrs. Weed. "I was telling . . ."

"Michael," I said.

"About his downspouts . . ." She went on and on.

Mr. Weed tapped me on the arm and traced a box in the air with his palms. "It's all one piece," he said with pride, but soft enough not to interrupt his wife. "Used four-gauge sheet metal, tack-welded it in the corners. Used the press at work. Can't even see the lap joints."

I couldn't help thinking that it looked like something you'd bury an animal in.

"That thing's over forty years old," he said. "Lasted longer than the wooden handles. Handles fell right off one day."

It didn't take long to find out why they set the *cofanetto* where they did. We lived near tracks and when the freights rumbled by, traffic would jam up for miles. People would turn down our street, thinking it went through to the viaduct, only to find a dead end. So they'd three-point turn into and out of our driveways.

I imagined Mrs. Weed cursing them each time. "Goddamn nuisances," she probably said. "I'll show 'em."

And they'd lived there twenty-seven years! I wondered how long she'd been ordering poor Mr. Weed to block the driveway, how long she'd been worrying about her air space. It had to start somewhere, sometime.

A week or so before the Weeds disappeared I heard them from my bathroom window, which faced their driveway. I felt I got to know them better on the pot than face-to-face.

"Goddamn idiot," she said to him. "How many goddamn times do I have to tell you. Put the parking brake on. Leave the brake on. I guess it's just too goddamn complicated for you."

Mr. Weed's job was to start and warm up the car, an old, pewter-colored, manual transmission Rambler with the stick right on the wheel. Then Mrs. Weed would march out of the house and plop down behind the wheel. The gears would grind as she worked the clutch and searched for reverse. Then she craned her neck and peered over the rims of her glasses, studying the rearview mirror, the back tires swerving on and off their driveway, on and off my lawn.

"I did put the brake on," Mr. Weed said.

"I'll break you," she said.

He mumbled something. If anyone else had heard him, they'd have said, "Poor Mr. Weed," but I sensed a certain dignity in it, too. He was beaten, sure, without hope of ever turning this thing around—short of shooting her—but he refused to become riled about it.

As the car pulled out, I turned to flush but stopped. Outside, tires screeched and metal crunched metal. I ran out as fast as I could.

Mrs. Weed examined the damage to the rear panel on the passenger side of her car. The other driver, a lanky man with a bristly mustache and a marijuana-leaf tattoo on his arm, stood behind her, his hands on his head.

"I was sure you saw me, lady," he said.

"Goddamn lunatics," she said. "I knew this would happen. Come speeding around that corner."

Mr. Weed was still in the car. His head was down and he seemed to be rubbing his windpipe. I ran to open his door.

"Need some air," he said.

My God, I thought. We need an ambulance.

"This goddamn emphysema," he said. He coughed and got out of the car. He glanced at his wife, saw that she was okay, and turned to his house. "Need some water," he said.

The dignity I'd sensed earlier had disappeared. She could have killed him.

"She could have killed him," I told Gale later.

"But everyone was okay?" she said. She sat in the family room reading some craft magazine. She'd been taking classes lately, and I worried that she would start bringing home a different toilet seat cover each month, one for each holiday maybe.

I slipped the magazine out of her fingers, and she shot me a look, the don't-start-about-this-craft-business look, that if-I-didn't-take-care-of-the-house-it'd-look-like-shit look. That look. And she was right, I guess.

But it wasn't about the house. Not this time.

"She could have killed him," I said.

"Would you forget about her. Ever since we moved in you've been fussing about her. She's old. They're old." She grabbed the magazine. The space between her eyes at the bridge of her nose became pinched, not a good sign.

"She's killing him, I tell you."

"Yeah, yeah, I know. *Cofanetto*. His coffin. If it bothers you so much, why don't you just steal the thing?"

"It's not just that. You ever hear how she talks to him?"

"Maybe there's a reason. Louise across the street says she's sick."

"And that gives her the right."

"I didn't say that."

And then the Weeds disappeared. No sign of them. His *cofanetto* didn't move. Three days. Five days. Six. The picture window drapes didn't so much as flutter. I imagined yellow police ribbons stretched across their lawn, cordoning off the house, while investigators dug up Mrs. Weed's body. When I told Gale about my suspicions, she acted more upset with me than she really was. And though she would never admit it, I got her thinking.

Finally, one morning while leaving for the office, early, the sun wasn't even up, I saw a light on. At least one of them was alive. The light was coming from a small casement window in the basement. No curtains. No blinds. Just a greasy smattering of smudges along the edges of the pane. From my driveway I could see the battleship-gray concrete floor and the bottom of a steel support beam. An unfinished basement would be a good place to hide a body.

I took a step toward their house and suddenly stopped. There's something sinister about peeking into another person's window, especially in the dark of morning, in the dark of a moonless sky, the only light anywhere pouring out of a bare basement window.

I walked over, squatted down, still on my property more or less, and laid my hand on the grass like I was picking weeds. With a glance I took in the room: cobwebs in the corner, shelves full of dusty mason jars, crates packed with newspapers. In a darkened corner sat Mr. Weed. If it weren't for his hands, gesturing freely, I probably wouldn't have noticed him. Every time his hands moved, his mouth worked too. It was like watching a silent movie.

It reminded me of Papa, who would pace the living room or the kitchen, talking to himself, whispering really, but intense, like he was arguing with himself. I'd feel embarrassed for him and try to duck out of the room before he spotted me. He didn't need me around while he was talking to himself.

I walked back to the car, thinking about Papa and Mr. Weed talking to themselves, in the kitchen, in the basement, the only places where they could say things without being cut off by their wives. I knew then that his wife was alive—and only a little embarrassed to admit my disappointment. Why else would he be retreating to his corner cubbyhole?

When I finally saw her some days later—they were both outside bagging leaves—I still felt a trace of disappointment. I sat on my front stoop looking for signs that something had changed. I studied her wrists and ankles for rope marks, thinking maybe he'd bound and tortured her. Or, since I hadn't heard her yet, maybe he had cut out her tongue while she slept. But then she let him have it, her tongue clearly attached, and I had to settle for less fantastic reasons for their disappearance. She did look a little sickly, as if she'd lost a few pounds.

As she lashed out at him, I hoped she'd complain about the leaves from *my* trees that had landed on *her* property. She raked the leaves to the center of the lawn while the old man filled the bags. He worked slowly, and a huge mound of leaves soon piled up next to him.

"Goddamn, goddamn," she said. "I have to do everything." She threw down her rake and started for the pile, then stopped. "No, you finish," she said. She picked up the rake and stomped off to the back.

I'd seen enough. I decided to go for a ride. Somewhere. Anywhere.

I can't really explain why I did what I did next. I sat in my car in front of the old man's house and reached over to roll down the passenger window. I couldn't leave him there with all those leaves. "Hey—" I said. I didn't know what to call him, still didn't know his real name. "Mr. Weed," I said. Weed was close enough.

He looked up and stared at me with his sheepdog eyes. He pointed to himself and mouthed, "Me?"

I nodded, and he walked to the car. He bent down to look inside.

"Get in," I said. He was used to following orders, I figured.

He squinted at me like he hadn't heard. He pointed to the car.

I nodded and smiled and waved him in. I was his next door neighbor, someone who listened to his sheet metal stories, someone who'd helped him out of his smashed car one time. So he got in.

As I pulled away I thought about Gale and how she'd let me have it. I never think things through, she always told me, told me so often that, what the hell, I started to believe it. I'd kid her later that this was her doing. I looked back to make sure no one was chasing us, but we were clear. Just that brown mound of dead leaves, which looked puny now, like a scab on the dry lawn.

Mr. Weed's cheeks were blotchier than ever. A tangled web of capillaries was sprayed across the tip of his nose. His forehead was beaded with sweat. Otherwise, he seemed relaxed, looking out the window, his hands resting on his thighs, as if he were out for a Sunday afternoon drive.

We turned the corner, passed Main Street, passed West Avenue Boulevard, crossed the tollway bridge. The farther we went, the more I expected objections, questions at least, but he didn't complain.

"Plastic," he said. He rapped on his side of the dashboard. "Everything's plastic."

I thought he was taking in the trees and the blue sky, thinking maybe about a time when he was a kid and left home for ten, twelve hours without saying anything to anyone.

"I worked for GM once," he said. He told me about the assembly line, how everything was done by hand. He talked about every other job he'd had. The stories were new to me, but I could tell they were the same old stories, repeated any number of times to store clerks, mechanics, bank tellers, anyone who had to listen. The stories kept him going.

We ended up in the city, a couple of miles from my old neighborhood. There's something about going back there that gets my heart racing. But this was about the old man, not me, that much I knew, so I turned. I found out where he grew up, a few miles south and east, and headed there, ready to hear all about his old neighbors. I wanted to stop to call Gale, but it didn't seem right. Besides, she'd just walk over to Mrs. Weed and explain what there was to explain—I'd love to hear that—and ruin everything there was to ruin. Then again, I didn't want Mrs. Weed to have a cardiac attack. Each time I saw a phone, I slowed down, then convinced myself to wait one more phone. And Mr. Weed didn't seem to mind. I didn't know whether to admire him for his composure or feel sorry for him, as if he'd lost something.

"Billy's used to be there," he said when we reached Halsted. "Gum, candy, soda pop, bread, hot dogs. Name it, I could still tell you which aisle, though it looks like a bar now so you probably won't find any aisles."

I stopped the car, thinking he might want to get out, but he talked on and on: he was ten when Billy died and he never found out the new owner's name but the sign never changed, always said Billy's, and his mom sent him there for cigarettes, a nickel a pack back then. These were the facts of the neighborhood, the facts of his life. Things happened. Things didn't happen. He could have been talking about some stranger.

I looked out my own window. I could've listened to tired stories in front of my house. I turned off the engine. Here I was trying to do the old man a favor, risking— What was I risking? Gale would yell and criticize, but we'd been through worse. I would promise never to do it again, blah, blah, blah. And I wouldn't.

"Say," I said.

He went on about Billy's. Away from home, he knew this was his chance to talk.

"Say," I said louder.

He slowed down, then finally stopped when I tapped him on the arm.

"What's your name?" I said.

He looked at me, then back at the store. I thought he was going to ignore me and ramble on about Billy's. He looked at me again, his green eyes focusing, like he'd just gotten up, dazed, but annoyed, too, at being awakened.

I suddenly felt cramped in the car. The steering wheel seemed clammy. My pants stuck to the vinyl.

"I was just wondering, you see, what your name was."

"Chester," he said.

As he said it, I winced, praying he wouldn't start rambling so we could have a genuine conversation. But that was all he said.

"Chester," I said. We sat there for a while, gazing ahead through the layer of dusty film on the inside of the windshield. Though it was October, summer gnats and mosquitoes were still plastered and crusted along the bottom of the glass where the blades didn't reach.

"Chester. I like that. I don't think I've ever met a Chester."

"I suppose Chester was more common years ago," he said. And then he stopped. No lecture on names more common years ago. He fidgeted with the release on the seatbelt.

I turned toward him, resting my arm along the top of the seat. "When we first met," I said, "you introduced yourself by your last name. It seemed a little unusual to me."

"That was my wife," he said with a shrug, a hint of apology in his voice.

"She's really something," I said. I wanted to ask why he put up with her, why he didn't fight back. I wanted to slap him awake so he wouldn't have to talk to himself in the cellar. But he looked tired suddenly, more tired than I'd ever seen him, so I decided not to press.

"You have any kids?" I asked.

He let out a sigh and looked away. He rubbed his knees. "A daughter," he said.

"I think I've seen her. Is she the one with the white car?"

He thought about it. "No, no, no. That's the nurse. She comes once a week. My daughter lives in Arizona."

I noticed he hadn't used her name.

"Do you see her often?" I said.

He looked down at his fingers, then folded his arms awkwardly, one arm resting loosely on top of the other. He picked at one of the liver-colored age spots on his forearm, like it was a scab he wanted to peel off.

"We never see her," he said. And then, because he wasn't used to talking about her maybe, or worse, even thinking about her, he grinned. And held it. Held it so long it must have hurt.

"Years ago she would visit," he said. "She'd stay a week, ten days maybe. Seemed the minute she got to the house she was thinking about leaving. Maybe not leaving, but saying good-bye. And we didn't make it any easier. 'How could you move so far?' we'd say. 'How could you do that to us?'" He rubbed his throat like he needed water. "I guess she and I were alike. I could never stand good-byes either. You don't have to say good-bye if you don't say hello, I guess."

I tried to convince myself that this kind of talk was doing him some good. I got out of the car, walked around, and opened his door.

"Let's go," I said. I was getting good at ordering people around. But this time he didn't move. "Come on. Stretching the legs will do you some good."

He took in a few deep breaths like he was readying himself for a long hike, then finally got out.

We walked past a couple of redbrick three-flats. "Is that a school up ahead?" I asked. The building was set back about a hundred feet, with a playground in front.

He looked and looked and focused. "I don't recall a fence." As we got closer, he said, "That's my school, all right. I don't see why they would put up a fence though."

It was a chain-link wall, ten feet high, without a gate. To reach the school you'd have to walk around the block. We moved close to the fence, leaned on it, our fingers crimped around a few chain-link squares above our heads, and like two kids, we pressed our faces against the cold silver. It didn't look that much different from my own grade school: a blacktop playground, monkey bars, squares spray-painted on a sandstone wall of the school for fast-pitching strike zones.

"I wonder if we played the same games, you and I," I said.

He rattled the fence like he was jogging his memory.

"It was a long time ago," I said. And then, "Too long ago to remember." It was a challenge, a schoolyard dare, a version of one anyway. If we were kids, the dare would have been to climb the fence maybe, and jump off. But a story or two was all I wanted.

He stepped back, and I turned. His forehead and cheeks were lined red with ridiculous chain-link marks. His eyes glazed over and he stared past me.

"Of course, back then we didn't have the blacktop," he said, something like the usual timbre back in his voice. He started toward the car without me, a slight bounce in his step. I practically had to run to catch up as he described his version of kick-the-can, his hands a flurry, as if they were making the images in his head spill out of his mouth. He talked on and on until his words became a lull, a pleasant drone, as if he were spinning a thick, warm cocoon around himself.

I drove him back to his wife and her airspace. Although she'd batter him a while for going along, her woes would soon converge with past woes. Mr. Weed would retreat to his tiny space in the cellar with its cobwebs and stifling sewer must, the bare bulb above his head throwing a harsh shower of light onto the cold gray floor and mortared walls. And in his shadowed corner, Mr. Weed, forgetting for a while how cramped he felt, would humbly recount his past, times when willow trees reached the skies and sprawled across boundary lines unnoticed.

Fixing a Hole

JUSTINE

THE SUMMER BEFORE MY FATHER LEFT—I was nine then, a pig-tailed tomboy—we discovered woodchucks living beneath the shed in our backyard. Actually, my mother and I discovered them one morning while hanging wash. I'd start at the lower end of the line while Mother worked the high end, and when we met in the middle she'd chase me until I fell, then tickle me breathless. I suppose she thought she was being rompish, but she'd do the same thing every time, brushing me clean afterward. My father used to say she was as spontaneous as a water bill, but said it in a way that made us all laugh. That morning while squirming on the grass trying to pry her scrawny fingers off my stomach, I noticed something big and brown dart across the yard behind the woodshed. I must have grabbed her fingers hard because she suddenly stopped.

"What was that?" I said.

She pulled her hands away. "What?" she said. The worry lines around her eyes fanned out.

"It was huge. It ran over there."

"What? What ran?"

"I don't know. It looked like a beaver or something." I jumped up and started toward the shed.

"Wait," she said. She stepped in front of me and pulled me by the hand. I couldn't picture her hundred pounds protecting me from some snarling animal, but her grip was solid and her steps firm. Daddy called her a frail rail. He'd point to me and say, "Justy could probably wrestle you to the ground and pin you, Gale. So you better watch yourself, you'll see."

At the base of the shed was a gaping hole, a perfect circle, the mound of dirt around it packed smoothly, as if the hole had been bored by a huge, swift drill. Surrounding the mound was a pile of thick, dried-out branches from the sycamore in the backyard.

"Groundhogs," she muttered. She shook her head in resignation. "Never thought I'd see groundhogs around here." She bit down at the corner of her mouth, the line in her neck stiffening. "Never thought," she said.

She probably figured she'd gotten away from groundhogs and possums and skunks after she moved to Chicago from Boone, Iowa. She'd been a receptionist for an educational equipment company in Sioux City and my father, Michael, who worked for the globe division of Rand McNally, called on her company occasionally from Chicago. He got to know her through these calls and finally met her one time during a business trip. "I knew right away it was him," my mother liked to say. "He had this long face and sad doe eyes, ink-black hair pushed off to the side. It'd always fall down over his eyes and he'd be forever setting it back." She probably overlooked the pointed nose, the lumbering waddle, the severe slouch, as if he were hauling a sack of coal on his back. I imagine she saw him instead as a fine, starch-collared executive who bustled in and out of gleaming skyscrapers all day. And he probably saw her as a swan-necked farm girl who scrubbed clothes over a wooden washboard, despite her manicured fingers and coiffed brown hair.

That night after dinner, Mother ordered him to get rid of "those filthy animals." So he and I took the bus to the library to read about groundhogs—not so we could find how to get rid of them, but to learn as much as we could about our new boarders—what they ate, whether they were nocturnal, mating habits. I often look back on that night as a turning point in my life, as the first time I defied my mother in any way. As much as I tried to convince myself that my father was the defiant one, I knew I was his willing accomplice. When he left that winter, I was sure it was my fault, despite his apologies and explanations, his insistence that he and Mother were just different.

Not until I was much older did I begin to understand why he left, why, when Mother would assert herself, he'd become withdrawn and broody, almost like a teenager. I think it had something to do with his family. Although I don't remember my grandmother, who died when I was three, my father would talk about her all the time, the way she'd bully *nonno*. I guess my father was determined not to let the same thing happen to him.

Any minor disagreements with Mother was a sign, I think, that he was failing.

But they *were* different, my mother and father. I remember times when I'd be talking with my imaginary friends, long after most kids outgrow that sort of thing, and my father would sit down and talk to them as well. I think he was afraid I'd grow up without an imagination if he didn't encourage this. But Mother would pull me into the kitchen and say, "Can your friends help me bake these muffins?" She'd say it sweetly, as if she wanted to play too, but later add, "Gee, your imaginary friends aren't doing much, are they, Justine?" When Mother bought me a new dress, my father would make sure we'd play baseball or climb trees on the day I wore it, not to ruin it, but to show that the dress wasn't going to confine our activities. They couldn't even agree on my name. He wanted to name me Perla, which means pearl in Italian. He said pearls were lustrous, that no two were alike. But Mother complained that Perla wasn't even a name. Besides, she said, pearls are nothing more than the innards of smelly shellfish. Justine, on the other hand, meant "upright, just." Just what? my father always wanted to know.

My father and I never liked to use the card catalog. So we strolled up and down the aisles, stopping now and then to flip through books with intriguing titles. The ones he picked didn't always thrill me, but he always seemed interested in anything I pulled out.

By the time we found what we needed, a book called *Rodentia*, the familiar announcement came over the PA: "The library will close in fifteen minutes. Please check out any materials at the front desk now." But we ignored it, like we always did, two defiant bibliomaniacs, and continued reading even after they flicked the lights on and off. We knew they'd never click them off for good until they were sure the library was empty.

"Mr. Comingo, Justine, the library's closed now," whispered a short, squat woman.

"Let's go, Daddy," I whispered, grinning. It was our little joke, how the women would know us, how they would whisper even after the library was empty. Walking to the bus stop, we whispered and laughed the whole way.

I didn't see the woodchuck again until a week later, the same day my father lost his job. I was in front of our house chalking hopscotch squares on the sidewalk when I glanced up and saw someone shuffling down the street. It was only noon so I kept staring, thinking it would start looking like someone else. But the head was down and the slouch was unmistakable.

I ran to him. "Are you on vacation again?" I said, out of breath.

"Sort of." He looked ahead at our house. "Where's Mom?"

"Fixing lunch, I think."

"Did you see him?"

Him, we learned from *Rodentia,* was probably a woodchuck or beaver or marmot. They all dug deep, complicated burrows and they commonly inhabited the Midwest.

My father's eyes beamed. "Maybe we'll see him today."

I grinned, glad I had a partner for today's watch. Beyond taking an occasional peek behind the shed, none of my friends were willing to wait around for a possible glimpse. Instead of going inside, we slunk around back to look at the hole. As I was about to unfasten the gate, my father grabbed my hand.

"Look," he said.

I pushed my face against the gratings of the chain-link fence. Next to the sycamore was our woodchuck. He had a small head with granite-gray eyes, Koala bear ears, a sheen-brown coat covering his watermelon body. He looked bloated. We had looked at the pictures in our book so often by then, we knew immediately it wasn't a beaver or plains pocket gopher or yellow-bellied marmot.

"It's a woodchuck," I said quietly.

My father nodded. "And it's a her."

"How do you— Let's look closer," I said, and unlatched the gate. The moment I did this, Woody, as we came to call her, scampered off behind the shed. I ran to look, but she was gone.

As we walked into the house, my father asked a little too quickly, too loudly, "What's for lunch? There enough for me?"

My mother was stirring something with a wooden spoon and barely glanced up. "You did it, didn't you?" she said evenly, bitterly.

My father scratched his head and looked at me. I must have seemed confused because he sat down and pulled me into his arms.

"Daddy's got to look for another job, Justy," he said.

"What happened?" I said. I glanced at my mother who shook her head, her back to us. They'd already decided they weren't going to argue in front of me.

He started telling me about how they finished a big project at work and there was nothing left to do. He looked at me, but I could tell his words were meant for Mother. Years later I found out that my father made enough money selling that he'd work two or three years, quit or get himself fired—I suppose he vowed that neither a wife nor a boss was going to order him around—then find another job when we couldn't afford the insurance premiums. In the meantime, Mother worked part-time answering phones at Realty World.

"You'll find another job," I said confidently.

For the next few weeks, my father came home every day at about noon. He was supposed to be looking for a job, but I suspected that he went to the library on many of those days. He'd come home and ask me all kinds of questions when Mother was out of earshot, like he was afraid she'd suspect too if she heard him. "Did you know," he said one time, "that two hundred million years ago, the continents were one big mass, one giant pie. Geologists call it Pangaea. But underneath, three, four thousand miles below, the core got so hot that it broke apart this Pangaea into plates. And these plates have been shifting for millions of years. They're still shifting. That's why we have earthquakes." He ran to get the atlas to show me how the jagged edges of the continents fit together like a jigsaw puzzle. "See, see. They've shifted. Plate tectonics, they call it."

I don't think Mother had the same suspicions about the library, but she knew he wasn't searching very hard for a new job. I'd overhear her morning phone conversations with her sister, who still lived in Sioux City. Her voice would get twangy like her sister's and carry through the kitchen window to the backyard. "I swear, I don't know what to do anymore. He gets bored or somethin'. Says he wants a job with possibilities. Like he's gonna change the world . . . Yeah, I know. That was ten years ago." Then her voice broke. Between sobs, she said, "It don't sound so cute no more."

When she hung up, I went inside, trying to act surprised to catch her crying. I figured I should ask her what was wrong but shuffled up to her instead and hugged her. It made her cry harder at first, but soon she stopped and wiped her eyes, the mascara and blue liner smearing clownlike. She pushed away a few strands of hair that were matted to her face. Why don't you let Daddy see you crying? was what I wanted to say. If Daddy could just see you crying, everything would be okay.

The longer my father remained out of work, the more obsessed he seemed to become with watching Woody, wondering when she'd have her litter. Which must have been soon after we first saw her because she disappeared for a while. When we spotted her again, two chucks, about half her size, appeared also. We called the lighter one Chuck and the other Gray. They'd scamper in and out of bushes like kittens, the slightest noise startling them. After a while though, Woody disappeared for good.

One evening my father and I sliced open a couple of apples and set them down beside their dark hole. While we waited for Chuck and Gray to pop their heads out, we pulled up the picnic table and played cards. When they finally showed, my father started walking toward them, like he was going to pet them or talk to them. I had to hold him back.

"Did you ever have any pets, Dad?"

He shook his head, staring at Chuck and Gray. They were wrestling with an apple slice.

"So Chuck and Gray are like your first pets, huh?"

He broke out in a grin. "You know what, Perla?" He still called me that sometimes when we were alone, when he felt playful. He scratched at his chin as if he had a beard, which seemed to help him think. "I'll bet Woody's in there."

"But Dad—" We hadn't seen her in months. According to *Rodentia,* two months overdue now, woodchucks usually lived alone. She would have had her litter, weaned them, and taken off. Chuck or Gray would leave soon, too, I knew. It was their nature to be solitary.

He sauntered to the shed and squatted down. I followed and crept down so that our faces almost touched. His breath was steady and warm, his dark eyes glistening. We looked into the hole. I sniffed and took in their animal smell, rank and wonderful.

"Listen, Justy," he whispered. But it wasn't a library whisper. It felt like something important was going to happen, like we would hear something no other person had ever heard before.

"What?" I said.

"Shh."

I didn't hear anything, just the crickets humming fiercely in the juniper bushes.

"Hear it?" he said.

I sank closer to the ground, hugging my knees, my ear inches from the hole. I held my breath, held it till I got dizzy, straining to hear. Finally, I looked at him blankly.

"Woody's down there," he said. His eyes were shiny and wide as nickels, filled with wonder, my cue to play along in his game of pretend. But part of me believed that he really did hear something and this was his way of helping me.

"I hear her," I said, my face mimicking his.

"Listen . . . she's whistling," he said.

We'd read about the woodchuck's shrill whistle but had never heard it.

"And we thought she left," he said. "She wouldn't leave without her chucks."

"Chuck and Gray are whistling, too," I said, as seriously as I could.

"Uh-huh." He stood and I stared up at his towering figure. "You know," he said, "a chuck can burrow some really complex tunnels, snaking this way and that. What's to say that one of these tunnels isn't connected to another tunnel?" He gazed across at our neighbor's yard where there was an identical woodshed. "And maybe that tunnel is connected to still another," he said excitedly.

I felt my heart race at the possibilities.

"There could be a whole community down there," he said. But then his face went slack, and a strange sadness crept into his voice. "And everything's connected."

I grabbed his hand and pulled myself up. "It's all connected down there," I said. We stood there for a while not saying anything, the darkness closing in on us like a curtain, the leaves from the sycamore rustling in the night breeze.

I nudged his side with my elbow. "They probably have little houses down there," I said. "And stores and churches. Chuck and Gray probably have to go to school."

He smiled and took his hand away to muss my hair.

The day before we finally returned *Rodentia* to the library, I began tracing the pictures in the book. When Mother saw them, she said, "Those are real nice, Justine." But her jaw seemed set and stiff, her lips a thin line. "Why don't you draw some lilacs or daffodils, something colorful?"

I hadn't meant to upset her, and from that point on hid my sketches. When my father came home, he found the pictures and motioned with his head for me to come outside. "You draw these?" he asked. His eyes darted from picture to picture as he shuffled them between his fingers.

I pointed to some freehand ones I'd sketched. "Here's Chuck and Gray. I didn't even have to copy."

"And this looks like Woody," he said. "Can you draw more?" He looked like a boy with a bag full of Halloween treats.

I said sure, and a week later had over thirty drawings: Chuck and Gray in their underground homes, in our yard, in a neighbor's yard, at their underground post office, at the library, whispering—every day my father told me where to put them. Then he added words to the pictures. We called our book *The Adventures of Chuck and Gray*. Even though my pictures all looked pretty much alike, I was always eager for my father's next installment.

By the time we had Woody reunited with Chuck and Gray in their underground Laundromat, my mother had discovered our book. I heard them from my room that night, their voices loud and flat, as if coming from separate rooms.

"I don't know what to say to you anymore," she said.

My father mumbled something.

"You have to get rid of those filthy animals."

"They're harmless."

"They've staked out their territory. Any animal's dangerous once it's done that."

"I'm telling you, they're harmless."

"Even if they are, they're infested with ticks. I'm surprised ticks haven't sucked them dry yet. And before long you're going to get skunks and squirrels and who knows what else in that hole." And then she said something about rabies.

After that night I sensed an urgency in my father to finish our book. Although I knew he'd get a job sooner or later, and we'd have to add pages more slowly, it hadn't occurred to me before that there would be an end.

He told me to draw ten or fifteen pictures of Gray crawling through dirt tunnels. No canary-yellow laundries or cherry-red schools. Just Gray in the tunnels. I went through two or three black crayons. My father wrote that Gray took a wrong turn one day and found himself in unfamiliar territory. When he tried to return, his old pathways had become dead ends. After seeing him separated for seven or eight pages, I pleaded with my father to let him get through.

Gray never got back home, but my father did insert a sort of happy ending. Gray met up with some badgers who lived near a mountain blue lake, and they took him in and cleaned him, never worrying for a moment that he wasn't a badger. I felt cheated. I didn't know anything about badgers or mountain blue lakes. And I knew I wouldn't be asked to draw them.

The morning after we finished the book, my father pulled rakes, shovels, bikes, a toolbox, and our lawnmower out of the shed. All that remained was the pile of dirt that Chuck and Gray had made when burrowing under and up through the wooden floor.

"What are you doing?" I asked, peering in. It was dark inside, light from the overcast sky barely filtering through the thick gray film on the tiny windows above the door. It smelled like weed killer and gasoline and dirt.

He wouldn't look at me. "Just cleaning," he said. He filled the hole in the corner with the dirt from the pile and packed it down with a shovel, then covered the spot with a wide piece of plywood the size of half the floor.

"How are—" I said.

He pounded a nail into the plywood.

"How are Chuck—"

He pounded another nail. When it didn't catch, hitting only dirt beneath, he started to cuss but caught himself.

It was October and the days were already chilly. Chuck and Gray needed to hibernate soon. "Daddy," I said, stepping inside.

"Don't come in here, honey. It's filthy." His voice was dry and raspy, as if he'd swallowed a handful of dirt. He finished pounding and went around behind the shed to fill in that hole.

"How are they going to get out?" I said, my eyes welling up with tears.

He stopped shoveling and looked at me for the first time that morning. He started pulling me into his arms but looked at his hands and the soot on his T-shirt and stepped back. Instead, he squatted down and brought his nose to mine. I didn't care about getting dirty, I wanted to say.

"You know what?" he said softly. "I was pounding that floor pretty hard. You think Chuck and Gray would have stayed down there with all that racket?" He shook his head and forced a laugh. He butted his head softly against mine and kept doing it until he got me to look into his eyes and smile.

"But they're not going to be able to get back in," I said. "Where are they going to stay?"

"They'll be okay," he said and explained how they'd be forced now to run back to the forest preserve where they'd be happier. But his voice soon trailed off, not convinced himself, and I suddenly understood my mother's impatience when he put her off about finding a job.

Two days later I noticed that Chuck and Gray had dug another tunnel, the entrance a marvelous, deep cavity, the dirt around it black and fresh. Whenever I could, I threw an apple or a cauliflower bunch down the hole. The food would always be gone within hours, but I never caught even a glimpse of Chuck or Gray until weeks later.

My father decided to mow the lawn one last time before winter. I tagged along, hoping he wouldn't walk behind the shed. He scraped open the creaky doors, stepped in, then suddenly retreated. A metal pail crashed to the floor; a shovel banged against the pail. I poked my head in and saw Chuck and Gray scamper down the hole they had made through the new floor.

"Shit," my father said. He grabbed a broom and shoved the handle into the hole and worked at it like he was plunging a clogged drain.

"Run," I shouted through cupped hands, and realized right away how silly I sounded.

My father turned toward me and tried to mask his snarl with a grin. As he caught his breath, he stared beyond me at our house, as if he were a stranger seeing it for the first time, his eyes panning it, like he was touring each room in his mind.

I scanned the shed and saw the mess that Chuck and Gray had made. An overturned gas can, fallen rakes, bags of sand and concrete mix shredded open. I looked back at my father. His eyes were still fixed on the house, but now they seemed focused and desperate.

He walked past me to the garden hose and pulled it toward the shed. He shoveled some sand and concrete mix into the pail and added water until it became a wet slush. But it was too wet and he had to add more mix, too much mix, and now it was too dry. He couldn't seem to get it just right.

With a trowel he scooped a glob of mortar and tossed it into the hole where it fell with a splat. With each splat he said, "There," as if nothing were more satisfying than filling that hole. It was deeper than he expected and he had to mix concrete four more times. Done, he patched the hole behind the shed. He slapped his hands clean and straightened his back.

I suddenly felt queasy and ran inside. I ducked into the living room closet before Mother saw me and eased the door shut. It was pitch-dark in there, another world. I crouched down, hugged my knees and rocked. The room seemed to spin, and I sank deeper, safe and warm. I imagined snaking my way through secret passageways that opened up behind me. It was possible to go anywhere and not be stopped by dead ends. I remembered reading that during hibernation, the woodchuck would draw breath once every five minutes; the heart would beat once every minute. I slowed my breathing. I didn't want to feel anything.

I heard the door slam and my father walk in. Mother came down the stairs into the kitchen. The floor seemed to shift, dizzying me. I nudged open the door a crack.

"They came back," he said, his voice shaky, like a boy trying desperately to please his mom.

"Who?" she said.

He looked into the living room as if searching for me. "The chu— The woodchucks."

"I know," she said.

He turned to her. "What do you mean you know?"

"I know. I saw the hole."

"Why didn't you tell me?"

I couldn't see her face, but I could feel her roll her eyes. "I should've told you?"

He turned away from her and seemed to look for me. I shouted, "Here I am," but nothing came out, a silent scream. The floor seemed to shift again, like the plates of the earth ripping apart, and I had to touch down to make it stop.

He started toward the stairs. He would ransack the house until he found me, I thought. But he turned back and began pacing. He seemed intent on making things right with Mother and couldn't do it, I guessed, with me in the way.

"Anyway, I patched it up," he said. "Everything's cemented down."

Mother sat at the table and started separating the month's bills. "They'll just dig around the cement, you know," she said, without looking up.

He let out a tired sigh and glanced up the stairs, as if expecting me to come down.

Here I am. Here I am.

If he called me, I decided, I'd run to him. But he kept pacing, his steps now slow and deliberate, unsteady. As I sank lower, my head between my knees, my hands cradling my head, I thought I would suffocate unless I heard, "Justy . . . Justy?"

When he finally did call me—Mother was gone, upstairs in her bedroom—I waited until I could slip out unnoticed, and while slipping, breath held, heard the awful creak and groan of the floorboard as it gave way, ever so slightly, beneath my feet. And as the floor moved, I knew there was nothing I could do.

Deep Left

GIACOMO

STANDING DEEP IN LEFT I WAS TERRIFIED. The wide expanse of green separating me from the infield seemed cavernous, and Tommy Brandin in center, though he cheated toward left because of the pull hitter at the plate, was a county away. I've never been much of a power hitter—punching singles up the middle was my specialty— but I'd always taken great pride in my fielding. For the past fourteen years, except for the summer of the broken leg, I'd played on dozens of sixteen-inch softball leagues, no mitts, no metal cleats, and now played every Sunday morning with Krunch and every Wednesday night under the lights with a team we called Arc Monsters, named after Andy Week's uncanny ability to throw high lobs for strikes. My speed has always been average at best and maybe a step slower now with my gut, but I usually got a decent jump on the ball, and if I could get to it I'd catch it. I have these soft hands that give just enough when the line-drive leather slaps them. Not huge hands, but they cradle the ball. That Sunday morning, though, I'd already dropped two easy ones, one luckily landing foul, and I wanted no part in any more action.

I can't recall a day when I'd felt so young and so old at the same time. I was thirty-four, and that morning had relished pulling on softball pants and lacing cleats and stretching for the first game of the season. Exchanging warm-up tosses with Tommy, I felt nineteen, ready to play a double-header. After three innings, though, my hands quivered and my legs wanted to buckle after chasing a fly. And I couldn't seem to track the ball well. I'd get to it, but my steps were heavy and I couldn't quite lock the ball in my sights. I told myself I was just out of shape, which was true enough, but I started thinking.

After my second daughter, Char, was born I scaled back from five leagues to three and then to two—I drew the line there, I thought. But I knew that as I stood poised in left, *not wanting the ball,* that the game's grip on me was waning. Squinting hard toward home plate at a lefty who liked to drive the ball opposite field, namely to me, I talked myself out of playing another season. After all, I had two jobs. I'd been delivering newspapers to the breakfast spots in town since college and the four a.m. alarm was beginning to drain me. After college and a miserable stint as a salesman for a pharmaceutical firm where I started soliciting tips on alternative careers from customers, I enrolled in a two-year clinical psych program—maybe to give me a chance to analyze my own life—and now treated ten to fifteen clients, depending on which week it was, who came in with anxiety problems and mild bouts of depression, nothing too extreme. And Kelly and Char just needed me around more—sometimes I felt like the dentist whose kids' teeth are rotting away from neglect. Between pitches I glanced at the parking lot to see if my wife, Teri, had arrived yet with the girls—she needed to drop them off before leaving for Tommy's wife's baby shower—and I felt grateful that she'd missed most of the game.

During the next few weeks I slipped off to the park near the house whenever I could to work out, to regain whatever I could of my old self, and as I jogged around the oval track I pictured my old self intact, waiting at an intersection for a bus that I soon discovered would never stop. My legs were gone, my lungs had shrunk, and I'd never been informed that they'd been replaced. It seemed like a cruel joke. My game did improve some, but working so hard to achieve that took the fun out of it for me. Softball had been a natural part of nearly every summer I could remember, like the sun rising effortlessly each day, a boy's game, and now it had turned into a sweaty pursuit.

After each game I checked off the date on the schedule, wrote down the score so I could have some tangible marker of my last softball season, then counted the remaining games. Of course, I played well enough my last few games that I started to second-guess myself and wonder if I had another season or two left in me. I considered options like playing right field instead, where there was usually less ground to cover, but the ball sails out there so much differently, and I'd be back to square one. Or I could play second, or even catch. As well as I'd played at the end of the season, I just couldn't picture myself out in left again, and I knew I was done.

At the end of the season, when Teri decided to have a garage sale, I pored through my closet and dresser drawers and discovered about two dozen old softball T-shirts and jerseys with silk-screened team logos on the front and sponsor ads on the back—John's Pizza, Big Tap, Tap This, Eddie's Beef—all places we'd frequent after games, the whole team usually, a ritual I would sorely miss. We had Algonquin Funeral sponsor us one year 'cause they were willing to spring for jerseys and pants, but we weren't quite sure how to support them after games. I spread out the uniforms on the bed, various shades of reds and blues mainly, which reminded me of how I used to lay out my comic books when I was a kid. In this case, I hadn't set out to collect anything, but that's what I'd done nonetheless—collecting to preserve something that had already slipped away. I folded each one, piled them up, and set them on a table in the garage. It was easier than I might have guessed.

"What are those?" Teri asked.

She had on these short jeans that hugged her thighs and a peach tube top that always drove me crazy. It was past ten, the garage doors were down, the girls were already in bed, and I started picturing us entangled and sprawled across the two-sweaters-for-two-bucks table. But there was still of lot of sorting and pricing to do, and she wasn't as interested, not after two kids, so I knew my chances were slim. Once the idea stuck though, I had a tough time dismissing it. And we'd barely touched in weeks, mainly because she was half-asleep by the time I arrived home after work. But she was definitely alert now, perspiring even.

"What?" I asked.

"You're selling your jerseys?"

She came over, tucked the red marker she'd been using for prices behind her ear, and thumbed through my pile. "I don't even remember half these teams."

The herbal scent from her hair, pulled back in a tight ponytail, cut through the musty dryness of the garage.

"Remember this one?" I said, and held up a maroon jersey.

"Leisure Strokes. I still can't believe you used that."

"It's a baseball term. Nothing wrong with—"

"Yeah, right."

"Here, try it on." I draped it over her head and she pushed her arms through. "See, we could join a co-ed league. Whattya say?"

"We wouldn't be Leisure Strokes, I can promise you that."

And right there, Teri could have gone back to pricing the rest of our junk, and I could have saved my heat for a different time, maybe even later that night, and the little exchange about the shirts would have been a sweet pause in the frenetic race to get the kids to bed and set up the garage for the next morning, but I ruined that by pulling her in and squeezing in that manner she would find unmistakable. She sighed, like maybe she didn't think this was a good idea, but she gave in, more out of obligation than passion, I thought, but at that point I didn't care how we got started. We threw a sheet over the sweaters, made a bed of the table, and after a while we were both nineteen again, an idea in which I took great comfort.

It was around that time we started talking about vasectomies, snipping the little vessels that carried my genetic markers into the void of a future. Where did those millions of busy messengers go if not out? Would there be some catastrophic buildup inside my scrotum or wherever the hell they went until it exploded? What worried me most was the permanency of the operation, like a rite of passage into obsolescence.

"Why didn't you tell me you were, you know, fertile that night?"

"Well, I didn't think you were going to— Hell, you usually pull out. You were crazy that night."

"You're supposed to give me some warning—like *it's that time of month* or *we'd better be careful* or something."

"Why do I always have to be the one to worry about it?"

"You expect me to keep track of your body?"

"No, just to take some responsibility."

And that's when she slipped in the possibility of vasectomy. From the family room she got down the medical encyclopedia and there in the kitchen, amid steak knives and maple chopping blocks, we studied the step-by-step diagrams. A doctor would cut and fold back the vasa deferentia, the two tubes that connected the urethra to the scrotum, *my scrotum,* and the sperm would be sent, I guessed, back to their source, forlorn and rejected. It could take months before the sperm that had already passed through flushed themselves out, the last of the last, like bottom-of-the-ninth, on-deck hitters, unwittingly abandoned, taking their final swings.

"We could go back to condoms," I offered.

"Please. That's how I got pregnant the first two times."

Lately Teri had become more emboldened, it seemed, as if she were tired of staying home with the girls, an arrangement that both of us had fallen into without much discussion once Kelly arrived. A decision borne not so much out of expectation, or so I thought, but a decision that transcended every concern save what was best for our new daughter. This passive decision-making had become a pattern for us, one that I could coolly identify but never quite face or overcome, like getting stuck to the same fly strip over and over again. Add two kids to the mix and any flaws are compounded to ridiculous proportions.

"So you're complaining?" I said. "You wish we'd been more careful."

"I knew you would do that. I'm just saying that condoms aren't going to prevent anything. We're not that . . . disciplined. In case you haven't noticed."

I gazed at the flaccid penis in the illustration.

"I hate discipline," I said.

"That's why this little operation—look, it says here it's outpatient—the operation would, you know, work. We wouldn't have to worry about it."

"I know, I know. It just seems so unnatural."

"I'll tell you what, Jim." She made her fingers into scissors and snipped. "I'll do it myself. It'll be all natural."

"You'd enjoy that, wouldn't you?" I smiled, but she could see I wasn't that amused.

"Have you got your ego tied up in your little pecker down there? Is that it?"

This time I did laugh, loud enough to wake up the girls, probably because I'd never heard her say *little pecker* before. It was usually at this point, with a few jokes on the table, that the conversation stalled or drifted to other safer matters, like what would Kelly or Char think of another child.

I said, "What if five years down the road we decide—"

"What? To have another baby? We'll be changing diapers in our forties. Is that what you want?"

"There's more to it than—"

"Someone has to do it. Someone who's home. You're looking at her."

Actually I was looking at the illustrated scrotum again and felt my own start to tighten up. Teri had never sounded so disgruntled.

"So we're through? With kids? *Finito?*"

"Don't you think?" She gently closed the book, embarrassed maybe that she'd decided the matter on her own some time before.

"I don't know," I said.

She broke into a grin. "You want your boy, don't you? Someone to play ball with." She looked up and beyond me toward the clock. "You know, Kelly's got a pretty good arm."

I nodded. "She does," I said.

The idea of having a boy hadn't surfaced in my mind for some time, and I was surprised at how right Teri was. I wanted my boy. As silly as it sounded, I wanted a miniature of myself, someone who would understand me like no daughter could. I realized that part of this longing had to do with the feeble ties I had with my own father, ties that might have run deeper had we remained in his native Italy. I'd often pondered that scenario, Papa leading me by the hand through the old village, introducing me to the other men, showing me the important places, places that spoke of generations. But in America he had nothing to point to.

"What about the pill?" I said.

We'd already covered this ground, and Teri shot me a sidelong glance to express just that. Medications usually produced bizarre side effects in her, and she was afraid she'd grow a mustache or some grotesque appendage.

"So you think vasectomy, huh?" I asked.

She shrugged. "It seems like a simple operation really."

"And it doesn't affect—performance. Right?"

"Please—"

"Don't laugh."

"I'm not. Just the word . . . *performance*. Sounds so—"

"Ah, forget it."

"You don't have to perform for me, Jim."

I wasn't sure why, but I wanted to tell her right then that I wouldn't be playing softball anymore. I didn't let on though because I knew she'd be glad. She'd have the right reasons for feeling this way, too. I wouldn't need to split myself in so many directions, she'd say; I could spend more time at home. But she wouldn't understand, because I wouldn't let her, what giving up ball meant to me. I didn't fully understand myself. I knew it had something to do with the unwilling admission that my body wouldn't do the things I told it to, not like before at least. And I knew that a summer without softball would disconnect me somehow from my past. I didn't want to concede that, though I knew I would. I didn't want to pass a lighted field on an August night and see the left fielder slapping away a mosquito at the back of his neck, then leaning, readying himself for a long drive, and feel the stab of loss in my chest.

"I hate change," I said.

She smiled and gazed at me in that consoling way she had with Kelly and Char after they scraped a knee or misplaced a favorite bedtime animal. With that look I felt she knew me better than I knew myself. I'd never formed it into words until then, but I thought, *This nurturing in you I've always loved*. She probably knew already that I was quitting; she'd been to the games and saw the signs before I did maybe. She was surprised but not shocked when I brought my jerseys out to the garage that night. And the next morning when I shoved them in a box in a dusty corner, she pretended not to notice.

"Sometimes change is good," she said.

"Right," I said, sounding flippant, though I didn't mean to. "No, you're right."

She took my hand and led me into our bedroom, where we made love without protection because the timing now was safe, her period days away. My last chance to pass along my genetic markers, whatever their worth, occurred in the garage weeks ago, both Teri and I taken aback when we eventually found out that we'd made good on that last opportunity. The next day, I leafed through the Yellow Pages, found the urologist with the biggest ad, and made an appointment.

We walked lightly around each other for a few days. I knew she was uncomfortable feeling angry toward me over something like this—a faint heartbeat not unlike her own would be pulsating inside her soon—but I couldn't bring myself to console her because I knew her anger was right. I'd been selfish. That night in the garage I was full of risk because I sensed a door closing shut on me.

"You're funny. You know that," she said in bed.

"Oh, thanks."

I stared at the blades of the ceiling fan spinning lazily.

She said, "You find out we're pregnant and call a urologist the next day."

"Isn't that what we—"

She laughed. "C'mon. If I hadn't gotten pregnant, you would have taken a year."

I turned in toward her and brushed my fingers through her chestnut hair. "Maybe."

"What if we have another girl?" she asked.

I kissed her on the forehead. "That would be okay," I said. "You're not upset you got pregnant?"

"Upset?" She thought about it. "No. Not anymore. Apprehensive maybe. A little scared. We're going to run out of hands with three."

"You know you're beautiful when you're pregnant."

"Oh, please."

I knew better than to insist.

"I should have been more careful that night," I said. I placed my ear on her belly and waited for my apology to sink in. "But you know

what. Don't get . . . I have to admit"—I patted her on the stomach—
"I'm **not** sorry."

"I know," she said, and sighed. "I can't say I'm looking forward to
the next seven or eight months, but I'm not sorry either, I guess."

I turned over and gazed at the fan again. "I suppose I should cut
back somewhere. So I could spend more time around here."

"That would be nice," she said and yawned.

She wouldn't have seen my giving up softball as cutting back, so
I didn't say anything. I shut my eyes and felt myself starting to drift
off. I imagined myself in the outfield grass, waiting and waiting, Teri
stepping up to the plate full term, waving me in, telling me it was
time, but no matter how hard I tried I couldn't reach her. My legs
were putty.

I stirred myself awake, my heart racing, and glanced over at Teri,
who was already sleeping, the first trimester draining her as usual.
Restless, I got up, threw some clothes on, and walked around outside a while before deciding to head for Shabonna Park, where my
Wednesday-night league played. It was after midnight. The lights
were off, the humidity so thick it caught in my throat. I walked out
to left and stood facing the infield, but all I could see was blackness
ahead of me. I tore at the grass and inhaled its scent. If I wanted, I
could do this, I thought. One more season. That had always been the
dream—one more season, one more chance to recapture the thrill
of chasing down a soaring fly that seemed out of my grasp, peering
over my shoulder and closing in on it, reaching to feel the sizzle of
the ball as it grazed my fingertips, watching it nearly slip away, one

last stretch, a leap, then pulling in that leather package and tucking it away like a newborn to my chest. The image was so real I shook my head, my chest aching with longing. I started to run, raced to where I thought home plate might be, picking up speed with each sure step into the darkness, knowing that this old dream would keep me long after I reached home.

Treading Water

TERI

I COULD STAND IT I THINK IF it weren't for those moments when I have to wait. When it's 8:57 and I have to get Kelly to kindergarten by nine and I'm bent over holding up the arm of the car seat, waiting, Char, my three-year-old, slipping out of my grip to adjust her shoe, the baby crying for her damn pacifier—"C'mon, Char, get in. Now"—Kelly pleading for me to hurry 'cause she doesn't want to be late again—"Shush, Kelly. Char, let's go. Kelly, give Joni her plug"—and I'm holding open the car seat, immobile, and I see my life for what it is. Or when I'm leaving Dee's Grocery, Joni under one arm trying to pry open the bag in my other hand, Char and Kelly stooping to view the plastic rings and other gunk in the gumball machine—"Not now, Mommy doesn't have change"—and I'm holding open the glass door, feeling my arm strain from the weight of Joni and trying to keep her away from the bag—"Kelly, Char, I'm leaving"—and I hear the shrillness in my voice that I swore I wouldn't use anymore and I regret it; standing there, I regret it, but I snap—

"Kelly Elizabeth. Char Marie. Now"—and I sense the glances from other shoppers, imagine their pulses quickening in their embarrassment for me. Or even the more serene moments before bedtime when the lights are out and the overnight lamp is on and I'm slipping away after kissing Kelly and Char good night and inevitably get stopped by a request for water or another book or 'When will Daddy be home,' and I pause, feel my breath become more deliberate, answer calmly, intent as I am now to end their day on a peaceful note, promising myself as I walk out that tomorrow will be a better day.

An hour later is when Jim usually strolls in, around nine thirty, and asks about my day. I tell him there's a bird in the dryer vent and we got to school late again and Char is impossible and I think Joni is sick because I can't understand why else she follows me around and cries all day. He tries to seem interested and explains that Kelly went through the same stages, the other ones are just going through stages. Deal with it, in other words. I try to explain, I need to tell someone, but I can see he's tired. In the mornings he delivers bundles of newspapers to all the convenience and breakfast spots in town. He's been doing it since college and every year he says this is it, the last year, but it's hard to give up the eight or nine thousand. Afterward, four times a week, he does therapy from one to eight, mostly depression and anxiety, nothing too wacko. Problems in living, that's what his clients have, he says. Sometimes I think I should make an appointment.

"I think I'd like to try to go back to work," I say one night to his back as he bends to pull a plate of leftover chicken from the refrigerator.

He sets the plate down, gets a fork, and sits. "Oh," he says.

"I'm serious. I'm going crazy. Here all day."

"What'll you do?"

"I'll find something."

He nibbles slowly, like he's considering, but it's just the way he eats, always the last to finish. I've always enjoyed watching him, his jaw working oxlike, but now he reminds me of Joni chewing on the lamp cord after I told her not to touch it and then slap—right across the mouth—I lost it. For ten minutes she was bawling, and I let her sit there, crying along with her, into my hands, soundless sobs.

"It makes sense," I say. "You talk about how you want to spend more time with the kids. You talk about quitting the paper. Quit. I could work in the morning. Waitressing maybe. You could sleep late. Get up with the kids." And wipe their mouths and their butts. And dress them—though God knows how they'll look when you're through with them. I want to add that he should link up with a hospital or clinic so we can drop the million-dollar-plus insurance policy he has to carry. But I don't want to bruise his ego.

"I don't know," he says. "You really want to wait tables?"

"I said maybe. I was just trying to think of a morning job."

He puts down his fork and stretches his fingers, his gaze sweeping from one hand to the other. He pats the table several times in what could be rigid resolve, a formidable gesture in some men, but in Jim, the hands are meant to calm. "We'll see," the hands say, which means he'll ask me about my job search for a few days or until I seem cheery again, then forget we ever talked.

"Well," he says. "Make a few calls. See what you find." He lifts the fork. "What time did Joni wake up today?"

When the radio blares the day's weather at four a.m., I spring up out of a deep sleep and picture flames. I can't breathe. Jim rolls to his side and slaps the button. "Sorry," he whispers. "Kids must have been playing with the radio. You okay? Go back to sleep."

I lie down, but I can't get my breath back, just these shallow gasps that keep me from falling asleep again, thinking how I'll have to get up in two hours anyway and begin to unravel. When I finally doze off I start dreaming about swimming laps in my high school pool, and even in my sleep I know that the dream is a snapshot of my life, confined and getting nowhere. I swim harder anyway, straining to tread water, but the image is cut off by Joni's cries. I go in and plug in her pacifier, but before I'm out of the room she starts. I snatch her up before she wakes her sisters, tuck her in bed with me, and hand her the remote. She can't even say moo, but she knows how to turn on the TV. The televisions are on constantly, four of them, usually to some inane talk show, my only link to the outside. When the colors splash on the screen she turns to me in mock surprise and gurgles. I root my nose in her warm neck to tickle her and she squirms in delight. This is what it must have been like with just one. I can't remember.

I could stand one, I think. Maybe Joni with her pacifier and her gurgles and her soldier strides, like she owns the place. Or Kelly, who can read the newspaper and recite jokes on command. Or poor Char, who's learned to look cute because she doesn't get much of a chance to say anything. But this is one of my problems, playing stupid wishing games that get me feeling worse than I already feel. How could I even think about choosing? How can I resent them like that? Because that's what it must be, though I'll never admit it. And I won't admit regret. The most I'll admit to is anger, the kind that simmers and steams and never seems to dissipate, even when they're making me smile, because it's *they* who are making me smile, *they* who steal whole chunks of time from me, and there's no stopping them.

I snuggle closer to Joni and decide that, for today, it's okay if they jump on the bed, leave their clothes on the floor, drown their pancakes in syrup, gargle their juice and let it trickle down their chins. But they're up an hour and the old reflexes kick in.

"Kelly, you said you wanted cereal," I say. She's six but more often adopts her younger sister's whining.

"I do. But not this kind."

"Why didn't you pick another kind?"

"There is no other kind."

I glance at the open pantry, annoyed that they've left it open, bothered by my annoyance, and see six boxes of cereal. "There's no other cereal?"

"I don't like those kinds." She hugs her knees and glares.

Char, who has slurped down half her bowl, declares, "I don't want cereal ee-der." Her mouth full, she pushes the bowl away from her and crosses her arms. She lowers her brow in disdain. Joni, who could not have understood any of this, I think, bangs on the tray of her high chair and catches the lip of her bowl, sending the oatmeal dripping down her pajama top, down her leg. Her spoon clanks to the floor. For a moment, everything is still and, as through a dense mist, I detect the possibility for humor in all this, but I don't have the energy for it. I feel their eyes fixed on me. They'll follow my cue.

What almost sets me off is a quick glance at Jim's chair. If he were here, we might all erupt in laughter—there'd be that possibility—and there'd be two of us cleaning up and I must be a terrible mother for not being able to handle this, but it should be my chair that's empty not his.

I force a smile. "It's okay," I say. "We'll just have to eat Joni's pajamas. What do you think?" But none of this wins them over or causes even a chuckle. Kelly and Char look away to the TV. Joni kneads the oatmeal, smears it down her pajamas, brushes her hair with it.

"Joni, no," I say quietly, gently, I hope. As I'm wiping her, I see Char out of the corner of my eye. In her little hands is the gallon jug of milk, which she's tipped and maneuvered pretty well, but her bowl is full and she's still pouring.

"Char!"

"I'm just—"

"Char."

I reach over and yank the jug away from her. "Look what you did."

"I didn't do anything."

"You didn't do this?"

"I didn't do anything." She recoils, buries her head in her hands, and sinks in her chair.

I find myself arguing still, going back and forth with a three-year-old.

"Next time. Ask. You don't pour milk. You ask Mommy."

That's right. Stifle her initiative. Make her feel worthless. I'm good at that. Forget about the unconditional support that the books talk about. It's not in me though. I always thought it was. Having three kids has shown me, like nothing else could have, my meanness, the kind I used to reserve for my own mother when she would try to tell me what to do. But I controlled it better then. Or maybe I didn't think I could hurt her; she could take it. She deserved it. But now, with my own kids, I can't see my way out.

Midmorning Jim stops home for a shower before heading for the office, and when he realizes that Kelly's at kindergarten, Char's at preschool, and Joni's napping, he starts pawing at me. I feel fat, bloated fat. I'm thinking, Let me diet first. Why do you want to do this? Let's do it later. When it's dark. His hot breath blends in with all the other snivelly demands of the day. I don't want to be touched. But he doesn't pick up on the signs and coaxes me into the shower with him. We're standing in the tub with our clothes on, and while kissing my neck, he strips to his underwear, which he likes to save for me. He starts to unfasten my bra and I reach behind me to turn on the shower, the cold water soaking my T-shirt and sweatpants, which arouses him, though I don't mean it to. I don't want to take my clothes off, is all. And I figure the cold water might douse him.

We manage finally to strip down and it turns out to be peaceful actually, holding each other, the stream from the showerhead pulsating in time to our movements, muffling the other sounds of the house. I tighten my embrace and close my eyes. I feel like my old self again. Whole. Not so much because of Jim—in fact, I feel oddly alone—but because I can forget about *them* for a while. I'm afraid to let go, like this feeling is going to leave.

For some reason, out of my control, it seems, my old self sticks with me the rest of the day and into the night, when Char cries out in her sleep. If I don't wake her she'll groan till morning, so I carry her into the living room. I pull a chair close to the window and sit there cradling her, gazing up at the waxy moon. Silver-blue puffs of clouds blanket it for a moment, then lazily pass.

Char stirs.

"It's okay, honey," I whisper. I pull her closer to me. "Did you have a bad dream?"

Her eyes are swollen with sleep. She swallows like she's thirsty. I stroke her hair, pushing it away from her face.

"Did you have a bad dream?"

She breathes now through her mouth.

"What did you dream about, honey?"

She swallows again and fingers the frilled neckline of my nightgown.

"Look at the moon, Char. It's pretty, isn't it?"

She looks and nods. Her brown eyes shine.

"I went to the moon once," I say. She rubs her eyes. "When I was a little girl." Silence. "Can you believe that Mommy was a little girl one time?"

She glances at me, a quizzical look spreading across her face. I can go to the moon, but not have a past. I'm puzzled myself in a way, since I haven't pulled back to think about it in so long, as if failing to remember the past wipes it away somehow. Innocence comes to mind. Not just my memory of it. Real innocence. Running on tall grass. The flutter of a new dress as I twirl to make it rise. The smell of thick yellow school pencils.

A surge of panic rises up in me as I imagine Char grown up and thinking back to her childhood, only to find spilled milk and icy stares from her mother. She shifts and settles herself, her fingers curled around my shoulders, and breathes evenly. I rock her and pray that the rocking will be one of her memories. I can give her that. And I can give her the smell of my hair and the touch of my hand on her head, the whispers, the moonlight. I feel, at least for the moment, as I wait for Jim's alarm, like I have something to give.

Trace

GIACOMO

THE FIRST TIME I STEPPED INTO LUANNE'S and spotted the cherry red floor cooler with the frosted glass doors on top that slid open with the push of a thumb to reveal a clump of ten-ounce bottles of Cokes and Nehi Grapes and brown-glassed Dad's Old Fashioned root beers that you could pop open with a flick of the wrist using the metal, jawlike claw attached to the side of the cooler, I knew I liked the place. Luanne had attached a small tin beneath the bottle opener to collect the metal tops, and the sound of the *plink* as the bottle top splashed down brought me back thirty years.

Until that March, Luanne's had been a dark, five a.m. stop where I'd toss my *Sun-Times* bundle at the front stoop and move on. But I changed my route, as I usually do once a year or so, and by the time I reached Luanne's at seven, my body was aching for her $1.99 special of scrambled eggs, fried onions, hash browns, toast, and fresh roasted coffee. It wasn't until I met Trace though that I started to anticipate those visits with a fervor I found embarrassing. She'd sat through high school commencement exercises on a Sunday and began waitressing for Luanne the next day, gliding from table to table with the assurance of one of the regular girls, slipping a pencil behind her ear and tucking her order pad in the pocket of that bubble gum pink uniform, which she'd smooth out each time after setting down an order, pushing out the supple contours beneath the stiff fabric.

I knew immediately why I was attracted. She had my wife's chestnut hair and broad smile that, unlike Teri, she didn't try to cover up. Her eyes were more emerald green than aqua blue, but she stepped with the same pigeon-toed lilt that struck me as uncanny. Here was a younger Teri I barely knew who occupied my thoughts more than I wanted to admit. I found myself projecting Teri's qualities onto this younger version, who liked to slip a tight white headband in her hair the way Teri once did. Trace, I decided, was great with kids and had a big heart and easily forgave and loved to laugh; and my stupid jokes wouldn't seem old to her.

Waiting for my breakfast special, I watched Trace smooth the sides of her tapered pink dress, which if it weren't for the distracted expression in her eyes, might seem like preening. Once I let on that three or four evenings a week I also counseled clients with anxiety and depression, she started to spend more and more time at my table. Here was someone finally who could understand her.

"So you're a therapist?" she asked.

"I counsel clients, yes." Even after a decade of counseling I still felt uncomfortable with *I am a therapist,* as if with that title

I stood on higher ground and could guarantee anything, as if I could fix others. *I counsel clients* seemed more innocuous and far more accurate.

She mainly wanted to talk about her boyfriend, Craig, who had also graduated from West and who apparently had no plans of any sort. Most mornings after she poured my coffee and we talked about the clouds moving in or moving out and how busy Luanne's had been that morning, I looked up and held my gaze on her longer than I knew I should, studied her stained name tag to avert her own gaze, and asked, "So, how's Craig?" I'd glance up again, and her eyes would tell me immediately if they'd been fighting or if he'd been taking her for granted or if she couldn't wait till her shift was over so she could hold him.

"So the two of you are getting pretty serious, huh?" I said one morning after she'd shown me her pre-engagement ring, a simple band with an amethyst stone.

She set down the coffeepot, continued to grip the handle, and leaned into her other hand, which she'd wedged on her hip, a position as close to sitting as she could come while she worked. She tried to hold back a grin.

"I suppose," she said.

"What are your plans?" I said, trying to sound more like friend than father.

"We're not sure," she said, her voice full of hope; the particulars would fall into place soon enough.

Between us, Teri and I had saved about $7,000 before getting married, and I envied the defiance against all odds that someone would need to become pre-engaged, whatever that meant, with no cash and no prospects.

"It's kind of exciting, isn't it?" I asked, genuinely curious.

"Well, yeah."

"Have you told your mom?" Her father, I'd learned, had taken off years ago.

A pained look crossed her face, and I wanted to kick myself. I hadn't meant to spoil her good news.

"Not yet," she said. "We will."

I hadn't forgotten that the ties between her and her mom were frequently strained, but I'd never connected that with Craig. Stupid, I thought, the same conclusion I often reached about myself during counseling sessions. I was forever being humbled.

"You know moms," I said. "They're . . . concerned. Maybe too much."

She straightened up, squeezed my shoulder, and smoothed her dress. Apparently I'd said the right thing or uttered it in such a way as to provide comfort. I wanted to return the touch.

She forced a smile and turned. "I'll be back with your eggs, Jim."

Some hours later, having returned the *Times* truck to dispatch, I sat on my front stoop, a slab of cold concrete, and daydreamed. Teri had gone off somewhere with the girls without leaving a note, which meant that I probably had the rest of the morning to myself. I checked my watch and imagined Trace punching out in fifteen minutes, swinging her mom's old cream-colored Lincoln out of Luanne's lot and pulling into my driveway to pick me up for a morning drive through sun-dappled streets on the far side of town. The Lincoln didn't get very far because it pulled up next to Teri and the girls, and before I could sink down they spotted me, bewildered by my sheepish grin and hunched shoulders. I was beyond pathetic. I couldn't even fantasize without getting caught.

My brother, Michael, was between jobs again, so I drove to his house and found him in the backyard reading about Garibaldi. Though he never finished college, he'd become a professional student, spending whole mornings and afternoons at the library, sometimes dragging along his daughter, Justine. Having inherited Papa's complacency about making money and a love for the old country, Michael had become Mr. Italian-American, an obnoxious expert on assimilation, language, the homeland, and whatever other topic he could lure you into. Every year he sent me subscriptions to various Italian-American publications in the Chicago area, expecting these pages to stoke up the same enthusiasm in me. The only time that the old Michael emerged was when we discussed women.

"She's how old?" he wanted to know. He stretched out in his chaise longue and put his hands behind his head. It was like gazing at Papa, all arms and legs, the same sharply cut chin, the same dark lashes.

"Nineteen," I said.

"Almost jailbait, Jimmy."

"Almost." We knew we were just two guys talking, that neither one of us intended to follow up on any of this talk. At least that's how it had always been.

"Stop by one morning. I'm telling you, she looks just like Teri. A younger Teri."

"Maybe she could use some . . . counseling!"

I laughed but felt something bitter rise up in my throat. Ordinarily we'd go back and forth for a while like that, but I drew back.

"I'm obsessed. I don't get it. I look at her at breakfast and think, I have that at home, I have the real thing at home, the things that attract me, yet—"

"It's not enough?"

"I don't know."

He sat up and turned and put his feet on the ground. "Maybe what you're really missing is Teri. How it used to be. Before kids. Maybe it has nothing to do with this young thing that waits on you."

"Could be," I said, and considered. "Or . . ."

"What?"

"I was just thinking. It could be that men and women aren't meant to be, you know, monogamous."

He shook his head. "She must really be something," he said.

That night, before drifting off, I saw Trace straddled over me, the straps of her ivory bra slipping down off her shoulders, the lacy cups peeling away in delicate little spurts and falling to my lips. When I woke the next morning at four, lying there waiting for the second alarm to sound after having hit the snooze button, that soft lace still real before me, I thought, these urges have nothing to do with Teri. These urges don't diminish what we have. I remained convinced of this for a good hour or two, after which I felt like a weasel and a lying snake, even though I hadn't done anything. I considered whether I could live with myself as a snake.

"So how's Craig treating you?" I asked later that morning.

The fresh hickey beneath her collar, which I wouldn't have noticed had I not been peeking as she bent to pour coffee, told the story. They were still in the honeymoon stage of their pre-engagement. My guess was that they'd met that morning before her shift, that they couldn't wait, that it was safer to arrange that sort of activity in the predawn hours of the day. Or maybe I was thinking about my own schedule.

I looked her full in the face, determined to hold my gaze. She answered with a broad grin that said, Craig and I are better than fine. But in that grin I saw something else, too, and I realized finally why I was drawn to her still. There was something confidential in that smile and in the little half-wink that followed, a harmless flirtation. Which was probably how she saw me, as harmless. But if it weren't for the ring on my finger and the ring on hers, and forget the twenty-year age difference, she was telling me, I'd have a shot. I'd have a real shot.

The honeymoon lasted longer than I expected, a couple of months maybe, a time in which she barely mentioned Craig, as if she feared she'd ruin everything by talking about him. And, as I'd discovered during my evening sessions, there wasn't that much to say when the days ran smoothly. But then she became distracted, more than usual, confusing orders, backtracking between tables. Her smiles were tired and the quivering line between her eyes betrayed her worry. Though she still wore his ring, I stopped asking about Craig altogether, afraid I'd cross a mine that I couldn't deal with there at the table.

"I didn't think you were working today," I told her. "I missed your mom's boat."

She shot me a surprised look, then smiled, as if satisfied that I noticed. "Yeah, I got a ride this morning."

I leaned into my coffee and sipped. "Craig?" I asked.

She scratched the tip of her nose with her knuckle. "No, just a friend."

"Everything okay?"

She scanned the tables, smoothed her uniform, and topped off my cup with measured restraint.

"I'm not sure if—"

"You don't have to," I said. "Don't."

"I'm not sure I can talk about it. Not here."

My heart leaped. After twelve years of marriage I'd never stepped anywhere near that spidery crack of opportunity that gave way to parking lot phone calls and one-hour motel reservations, later slipping into the house unnoticed, walking around in it for a while, *my own* house, trying to ground myself again before she read my face and discovered where I'd been, this woman with whom I had spent most of my adult life. Trace stood there ready to cry, waiting for me

to ask *Where*. Where *could* we meet? But I was lost in my own fever-
ish thoughts, trying to negotiate with myself, wondering if I could
have both.

She took in a careful breath. "Can we—talk somewhere, Jim?"

I thought, Sure, why not, but I'd lost my voice and managed only
a weasel of a nod.

We met after her shift. I backed into a space at the far end of
Luanne's lot so all anyone could see from the restaurant would be the
back of my head. No one there knew my car, I figured.

I drove to Shabonna, where I'd played softball for many years
under the lights, and we sat on a bench along the asphalt trail that
weaved through the park. Dandelions pushed through cracks in the
dry asphalt. Except for a few kids running up and down the steps
of the tan-brick field house, and one hunched old man walking the
path, the park was empty. I wondered if the man had ever reached
this point in his life, what he'd been through, what he'd decided. I
needed wisdom here. I needed perspective.

What surprised me most was how comfortable I felt sitting
there, tracking a dragonfly zipping overhead, taking in the sweet
scent of the newly mown grass. I could have taken her hand or
sidled up close or fixed my eyes on her without reservation. If
it were night and she were dressed in something other than her
pink uniform and she didn't smell all syrupy, I might have felt
differently.

"I think Craig and I are through," she said and began to cry.

I wanted to hold her. There was nothing wrong with consoling her. I moved close, touched her shoulder, and she sagged into my chest, tugging gently at my shirt.

I thought, When was the last time that Teri and I had shared an intimate moment like this?

Once she'd exhausted her sobs I pulled away and asked, "When?"

"A couple of weeks."

So she was vulnerable, on the rebound, as they said. Not a good time to be thinking of my own needs, but my pulse had quickened at her touch, and I could feel myself tremble.

"So what do you want to do?" I said.

"I don't know yet."

I looked at the old man swinging his arms contentedly. I wanted to yell over to him, Hey, you, old man . . . ever cheat on your wife? A part of me envied him, too; he knew his place. Even those kids bounding up and down the stairs, for the moment at least, were sure of their place.

"What happened?" I asked.

"He's been kind of distant. Ever since I told him."

"Told him?"

She fingered the hem line at her knees and stared at her flat white shoes. "That I'm pregnant," she said and looked up, the resignation in her eyes flashing at me like an apology.

"How far?"

"Two months, almost."

I trembled still and smiled weakly to hide it, embarrassed by how far I'd taken this in my head. I let out a slow sigh and knew that all I had to do was pull back and become more like a clinician and I'd be okay. In time I'd walk to my car, drop her off, and fall back to the routine I'd carved for myself and nearly toppled, grateful now that my affair had consisted of only a morning hug on a park bench.

After telling her about the numerous agencies that could assist her, some really good agencies that provided support more than advice, I patted her hand and shook my head.

"It's a mess, isn't it?" I said.

She nodded and worked up a smile and curled her fingers around mine. Her hand was smaller than I'd imagined. "Sorry to drag you into this," she said.

I felt sorry for her, truly sorry, thinking what Teri would have done at nineteen. She gave me one of those hoodwinked smirks that had given me hope at her table, but it melted now into a tired frown— her pregnancy was one obstacle we weren't going to surmount, not even in our harmless little exchanges at Luanne's.

We sat there a while longer holding hands, the old man passing before us, offering Trace a good-morning nod and glancing at me with a devilish grin, as if he knew my business there. Was I that transparent? Already feeling out of place, I looked away, not wanting to give him the satisfaction of returning the grin. I'll be going home to my wife soon, I wanted to tell him, and I won't see you here again. Until then, I'd sit there as long as I pleased, squinting hard to shield my eyes from the harsh sun, thinking of Michael's words, about how I'd been missing Teri, the way it used to be with us. I knew he was right when he told me. I was just looking for a way to hang on to what I had back then, to feel the way I once did, to go back to the place that I thought I could still get to.

Blood Lines

I

A S HE WATCHES HIS TWO GROWN sons stride into the shop, Fabio Comingo feels a familiar jab of grief. Nothing overwhelming— his wife, Lucia, is three years dead—yet it dizzies him for a moment. He stares beyond his sons at the barber pole, its blue and red stripes snaking into the pole's ornate, white dome, and the image of his sons as boys rises up before him like mist. They are sitting in the kitchen, waiting for one of their Sunday afternoon haircuts. Lucia is at the stove frying dough for *frittella*. He can taste the sugar she will sprinkle over it when the dough becomes crisp and golden. He hears her warnings about keeping the hair clippings away from the table, but he can't make out the face, just a swirl of dark hair as she darts from one end of the kitchen to the other, nothing more than a blur. When he thinks of her, she is rarely sitting. He sees the tops of his sons' small heads as they laugh conspiratorially. He sits behind them, his scissors ready, and takes in their playground smells: the leather of a football, the burned powder of spent firecrackers, bicycle-chain grease. The shop door wheezes shut and triggers a bell, which clinks and pushes the kitchen out of mind.

His younger son, Jim, sees the dreamy look in his father's eyes, a sign to Jim of listlessness, of a life lived with little drive, and he becomes immediately annoyed. He knows he will not say anything though, not in front of Michelino, who will play the tolerant, understanding older brother, especially today, the day before his fortieth birthday. As far back as he can remember, Jim, thirty-seven, has always felt like the older one, the one with his feet on the ground, the one with his head out of the clouds. They are alike, his father and brother Michael, and there was a time when he envied this, envied their closeness. Now, when he can look beyond his annoyance, he feels sorry for them. Michael didn't own his first house until he was thirty-six or thirty-seven, and even then it was just some tiny starter home in the middle of nowhere. Jim, on the other hand, is already on his third house. His father was sixty-two before he had his own shop again, and only because old man Bruno willed it to him and finally was gracious enough to die. At first, Jim was saddened that Mama never got to see her husband as an owner again in America—she never counted the time when he first arrived, a nine- or ten-month nosedive. But even if she were alive, she would laugh with contempt, complaining that Fabio should be shame-faced for taking so long to make something of himself. Between breaths, though, she'd be dialing a friend to brag about her husband's new shop, late in life maybe, but what an opportunity.

Michael, the taller, leaner one, doesn't notice his father's distant stare—and if he did, it would not annoy him. He is busy taking in the smells of powders and lotions and the scent of something like mint in the air. He remembers how, as a boy, he would count the black-and-white checkerboard tiles and try to form pictures out of the cream-colored flecks in them.

"Papa ," Michael says. "*Wileyo*. How are you?" He hugs his father, cuffs him on the neck, then steps back to view him from head to toe. He squeezes his shoulder and with his other hand pinches his father's taut stomach. "All muscle," he says. "You look good."

"Like twenty-five," Fabio says.

Jim feels the old trace of jealousy creep up as they ignore him, but it quickly passes. "Yeah, twenty-five. On one side," Jim says, beating his father to his old joke. He claps his father on the back, then sits in one of the two red-leather barber chairs. He has bulked up since his high school wrestling days, his stomach bulging out like a stuffed bean bag.

Michael plops down in the other chair. "When are you going to hire another barber?" he says before he can catch himself. He glances at his brother, his pudgy little brother, hoping he won't start. Jim's weight pleases Michael, particularly when Jim pesters him about finding a career, about sticking to one job at least, as if a career would make life a paint-by-number deal. Jim's weight is a reminder, Michael hopes, that some things are out of our control.

"It's a good idea, Pop," Jim says. "With this location, you'd fill the place." Even when the shop opens in an hour, it will still be more or less empty, Jim knows. The regulars will show up for a game or two of boccie out back, but none of them will open their wallets. When he and his brother built the alley, not long after Bruno died, the regulars, old crooked men with gnarled fingers, were quick to offer advice, but none of them picked up a hammer or offered to help pay for lumber or limestone. Mama would have had something to say about these stragglers—and about wasting money building the cursed alley.

"Hey, *mio fratello,* lighten up," Michael says. He laughs but he means it. He misses the days when, as boys, they would kid Mama, mimic her broken English, even if she were in the middle of a heated argument with Papa. Even as adults, during Thanksgiving and Christmas dinners, they would throw in their digs, Jim's remarks always a bit more cutting than Michael's, and they'd exchange knowing glances, furtive grins. When Mama died, their common target was gone, and they became serious, almost awkward, with each other. Her death forced them to look beyond the jokes, beyond Mama, which finally brought Papa into focus. And oddly enough, despite Jim's hard-edged stabs at Mama when she was alive, he now views Papa through *her* eyes.

"And so I fill the shop," Fabio says, and shrugs, his hands going out. He stands behind Jim, looks at him in the mirror, and shrugs again, more deliberately this time, unsure whether Jim noticed his nonchalance the first time, wishing that his son were less anxious. But he sees little hope in that. Even as a baby Jim was stubborn, unresponsive, not wanting to be held. He can accept his son's seriousness, but he wishes that Jim would stop pitying him.

"How are the girls?" Fabio says.

"Fine," Jim says. "They want to know why you don't cut their hair."

"You should have brought them," Fabio says.

He wanted to. Before he left the house, his eight-year old, Char, clambered playfully onto his leg, insisting that he bring her along. Kelly, four, spotted her and hopped on the other leg. But he knew that Michael, though he loved being around the girls, saw these morning haircuts as exclusive, a time for the last of the Comingo men to huddle around like warriors, as if this would magically preserve the family name. Lately *Michelino* has been trying again to convince Jim to go downtown to change Cummings to Comingo, like Michael and his father had done years ago. His father never seemed to have his heart in it though. If he had, Jim would have gone along. But it was just a name, and changing it would have been a hassle. It was easy for Michael; he didn't have any kids at the time. But Char was already a year old then. Michael's recent urgings puzzle him, too. Jim had three girls and a vasectomy, another reason he didn't bring the girls, a reminder of what he'd bred and his inability—his *unwillingness*—to do more. So with no hope of any boys on the way, what difference did it make what his name was? He is surprised that Michael hasn't fed him stats on the success of vasectomy reversals.

"And Justine?" Fabio asks.

"Good," Michael says. "We just checked out a book on Italia from the library. She wants to show you."

"She reads?"

As if in reflex, Michael and Jim glance at each other and smile.

Papa's remark would have triggered a story from Mama about her sixth-grade education.

"She's seven years old, Papa," Michael says.

Jim decides to rile his brother. "Did you get your passport yet?" he says, making no attempt to hide his sarcasm.

"You sure he's my brother, Papa?" He is tempted to comment on Jim's girth, an unusual Comingo feature. "He talks like a *buffone*."

"No, really. You're always talking about going back. He's always talking about going back, Pop."

"At least I'm interested," Michael says.

"What, I'm supposed to be proud because"—he doesn't want to hurt his father—"because I happen to be a particular ethnic persuasion?"

"Just say it. You hear what he's saying, Papa?"

Jim spreads the apron over his knees and sinks in the chair. "I just wanted to know if you got your passport."

"Oh, no. You're not getting out of this one," Michael says, pointing his finger. "He's embarrassed because he's Italian. *Italiano*. What do you think of that, Papa?"

Fabio is tired of thinking. He did enough thinking in forty-one years of marriage to last him the rest of his life. Although he misses Lucia, and although he is reluctant to admit it, he finds her absence liberating, invigorating even. "*Capo tosto,* both of you," he says.

"I never said I was embarrassed," Jim says. "I'm not proud is what I said. How can I take pride in what someone else has done? I take pride in my work, in my house, my car—things I've accomplished. I don't give two shits about the past."

"So I check out this book for Justy and talk about where her *nonno* comes from—where I was born for Chrissake—and her little eyes light up, she's asking questions, and I'm supposed to believe that pride has nothing to do with it."

"I'm not saying you shouldn't be proud." He wants to let it go, but he can't. "You're showing her pictures, maps, places—pieces of dirt. It's a coincidence that you were born there. Sure, you were born into a particular blood line, but that was all chance. The fact that you're even alive is a one in, what, five hundred million chance. If I win the lottery, I'm happy, sure, but I'm not proud 'cause I picked the right numbers. I was lucky."

"Ah, so that's why you got your vasectomy, huh?"

Jim shoots a look at his father, hoping *vasectomy* is not in his vocabulary. Fabio speaks English well, mainly from watching TV and reading the newspaper, but Jim usually knows how to phrase words in a peculiar way so as to hide their real meaning. Jim is fairly certain that his father will not be upset about the results of a vasectomy—his father has never made the typical jokes about the need to bear a son—but Jim is afraid that his father will view the tiny incisions as a betrayal. He'd think it unnatural, a violation of some code that says things should fall where they will.

"Papa . . . Hey, Papa ." Michael swings his chair around, reaches for a pair of scissors, and snips at his crotch. "He's a eunuch, Papa. Jimmy Cummings"—he spits out *Cummings* like it's distasteful—"is a eunuch."

"This is true?" Fabio says. He tries to act more concerned than he really is on Michelino's account.

"It's nothing, Pop."

"Yeah, nothing," Michael says. *"Niente."* He saunters over to his father and stands behind him. He is a head taller than his father, and, with Jim in the chair, the mirror reflects back to them a totem pole of faces. It would make a nice photograph, Michael thinks. What he wants to say next sits on his tongue like acid. He tries to swallow it and remain silent, but he's afraid he won't be able to stop himself. He grabs his father's shoulders, squeezes them. *"Si,* Papa. It's nothing," he says softly. "A little snip. Maybe you should have had it done after I was born." The remark, once uttered, sounds less inflammatory than he feared. Coming from Michael, it turns out to be just the right thing to say.

Fabio stops the scissors and places his hands on Jim's shoulders. They remain there for a while like that, still, only their eyes roving up and down, each of them thinking they'd like to freeze this moment and tuck it away for safekeeping, this image of the three of them together.

2

FABIO

There have not been enough moments like this in my life. I am in my own shop, my hands on the shoulders of one son who is silenced by the words of the other son standing behind me, touching me, who cannot be mean even when he intends it. His words, as usual, have a way of neutralizing the bitterness in the air. The time I left Lucia for a night, Michelino, eleven years old then, and Giacomo, they walked into the shop the next day, and Michelino said, "Mama's crying." That was all he said, all he needed to say. The three of us walked home. When we arrived, Lucia of course had finished her crying and seemed ready to fight again—she could not help herself—but Michelino knew how to quiet her with his banter.

Giacomo has a good heart as well, but it is harder to penetrate. He has inherited Lucia's ferocity, which when aimed at work benefits him greatly. I suspect that he earns more in a year than I do in five, though he would never tell me this. Each time he moves into a new house or buys a big car, he is embarrassed, as if this will show up and shame his poor father. But my pride for him, for his accomplishments, which I have never hidden, is genuine. It is true when they say that a parent wants better for his children. Giacomo will understand someday.

But he is still a boy in many ways. When he comes to the house, to check up on me I think, usually at nine or ten o'clock in the evening, I am sitting in the recliner, the one he gave me at Christmas, in the dark except for the glow of the television, watching dancing girls on the Spanish station. I would watch Italian if it were on. I am resting, tired, lonely sometimes. I still miss Lucia.

"Hey, Pop," he always says. "What are you watching?"

Then he picks up the remote control and changes the channel, not to what he wants, but to what he thinks I like, or should like.

"Why is it so dark in here?" he asks. He runs to the kitchen first and turns on the light, checks the food in the refrigerator, which must seem meager to him without Lucia here to fill it. "I can't believe how dark it is in here, Pop." He walks through the rest of the house, flicking on lamps, wall switches, until the entire house is washed in light.

And like Lucia, he does not sit. He reads my mail, warns me against senior citizen insurance brochures; he checks the thermostat, the clocks; he tries again to teach me how to use the video cassette recorder, another gift. I can rent Italian movies, he tells me.

Michelino comes over, too, and together in the dark we sit and watch the girls on television flare their legs above their heads. He pours himself a glass of wine from my homemade batch, the first I have made in years. Sometimes he asks me about Italia, but mainly we relax, enjoy each other's company, enjoy the darkness that seals us, that sends me back to our old apartment when Lucia would work nights, and Michelino and Giacomo and I would watch Red Skelton or Jack Benny.

I often imagine Lucia walking through the living room, picture her stomping through the house, vigorous as ever, turning on lights, complaining, her face coiled into a tight grimace. "Why is it so dark in here?" she says. Then I hand her the remote. Other times I imagine her slipping into the house, sharing the dark with me, sitting on the couch, reclined, like she did near the end, the last month or so, when the cancer had completely overtaken her, when she had finally stopped fighting and decided to relish, whenever possible, whenever the pain would loosen its grip, whatever time remained. I see her face. Her cheeks sag, though the skin, I know, is baby-soft. The bruiselike circles around her eyes make her wilted head appear smaller, more skeletal. Yet she is placid. In forty-one years of marriage I learned to put up with and even love the stomping Lucia, but I prefer to preserve this image of the quieter, composed woman on the couch, even though the composure was forced upon her by disease. The cancer gave her dignity, allowed her to sit. It taught her finally to let go. And watching her, with an eye on my own remaining years, I learned not to be afraid.

3

GIACOMO

I see his point. I really do. But he makes the snip, as he calls it, sound like the most selfish procedure known to man, on the level of taking a sniper shot at the pope. He doesn't understand how not having a vasectomy could also be selfish. I love my kids, but I really don't want any more, and I don't think I could hide that from a fourth child.

I'm not sure I understand Michael's motivation all the time, but I do understand and feel his anguish. Justy was no problem for his wife, Gale, but then she had three miscarriages, all within a couple of years. It put a strain on the marriage, and then Gale said, No more. She wouldn't go through it again. Instead of feeling lucky that they'd been through three miscarriages and not four—they did have Justy— my brother became even more broody than usual. He became angry with Gale. They were both going through this thing, he said. They were both hurting. But turning their backs wouldn't lessen or erase the hurt, he argued. Which struck me as illogical. Turning away in this case seemed exactly the right thing to do. And I think Gale saw the irony: turning away—from responsibilities, from jobs—was what my brother did best.

I hope, pray sometimes, that he doesn't walk out of his marriage. His obsession with the old country, with its quaint codes that forbid divorce, should, but won't, guarantee that he stays. But hopefully he stays for the right reasons. Despite his claims to the contrary, he's an American, and smart enough to realize that forbidding divorce often leads to the condoning of affairs. In many ways, Michael is a sad replica of my father.

But Papa, of course, never became Americanized. He was always naive enough to believe in the old ways. As a teenager I often wished that he would divorce Mama, thought that it would be healthy for the two of them. But I knew he couldn't. It was mostly my own selfish longing to escape that nagged me anyway. I'm not proud to admit it, and I wish it didn't still curse me today, but I had to be selfish. I had to stake out my territory, even when it meant lying to Mama and sometimes to Papa. What other choice did I have? Fight, and Mama would have squashed me, at least that's what I thought then. Go along like a worm, and end up like my brother.

I have to hand it to Papa. He survived. Endured, at least. And never complained, though Mama didn't allow much room for that. I even remember moments of tenderness between them, Mama pinching his cheek, running her fingers through his thinning hair, Papa squeezing her shoulder, pulling her from the stove and guiding her to a chair. Sit, Lucia, he'd say. Join us. Or the two of them posing for snapshots, rigid like strangers because they hated being photographed, but intimate with each other's curling fingers. I see now, as Papa stands sandwiched between his two sons, that he misses her deeply. I would have never guessed it.

4

MICHELINO

As the three of us stare at our reflection in Papa's mirror, I see out of the corner of my eye a woman wearing a dark babushka walking by the shop. She moves fast, probably to get to the grocery store on this Saturday morning. Just as she's about to disappear, I'm tempted to break my gaze, turn, and look directly at her. But I close my eyes instead and imagine her to be Mama. For the briefest of moments, time is suspended, and I feel that the four of us are together again. And that Jimmy and Papa feel the same, but that none of us will ever be able to put these thoughts into words for each other.

We were never able. The words eluded us, literally, especially with Mama. They got tangled and jumbled and became near gibberish. Mama would ask, "School is okay today?" I might say, "Yeah, I got a form, *una carta* that you have to sign, *insegna, che dice che* it's okay to go on a field trip."

"Trip?"

"Field trip . . . to the museum. On a bus."

I knew enough Italian to convince her to sign the papers, but she'd seem surprised a week later when I needed money for the *viaggio,* the journey, I was taking at school. You'd think that someone in the family would have thought back then to buy an Italian/ English dictionary at least. Jimmy and I felt like tourists at times, trying to convey our intentions with our hands and pictures and mangled translations. I don't know, maybe we all hid behind this language barrier after a while. Rather than talk about what was really going on at school, it was easier to find the simplest translation and be satisfied that Mama had a general idea of what you meant, even if it wasn't accurate. And it made it easy to con her, which Jimmy, especially, seemed to take advantage of. If he knew Mama didn't approve of a friend, he lied about going to his house, probably convincing himself that she wouldn't understand him anyway.

And forget about mentioning your feelings. That would have been like cracking a code for her. But like I said, maybe we used this as an excuse. Maybe we were worried that Mama *would* understand.

Though Papa learned English fairly well, this didn't make it any easier to talk with him. Mainly because he preferred not to talk much at all. The only time he became animated, boisterous, was during boccie matches. He'd cuss and shout with the rest of them as the balls collided and crashed, with such force that had they been aimed at someone, they'd have knocked the person off his feet. Somewhere along the way Papa had become amazingly accurate, his ball zipping, cutting the air, landing and pushing out an opponent's ball forty feet away.

When I did try to talk to him, with complaints about Mama, he listened and nodded, never tried to laugh off my complaints, but I could tell he felt like he was betraying his wife by not taking her side. He walked the fence. So we never got anywhere. Not until the end.

Mama was diagnosed with colon cancer in July and was dead in January. When she first found out about the cancer she reluctantly agreed to chemo, but it made her so nauseous that she simply stopped going to the hospital after a few treatments. The doctors don't know anything, she said. All they want is money money money. The only time she went back to them was for morphine to dull the pain. In the meantime she battled the cancer with homemade brews and elixirs, concoctions her mother must have used during fevers and colds and sore throats. I think she believed that if she treated the tumor like these other ailments, it would shrink and actually transform itself into a cold or fever.

I never realized she was so superstitious. She drank chamomile tea dashed with a sprig of mint leaves at every meal. Her intake of garlic tripled. She performed these bizarre rituals to relieve her pain, like sticking the top of a drinking glass to her stomach and lighting the bottom of the glass with a match. She claimed that this would suck out the pain. When she came to this country, Mama was always determined to fit in, to hide her origins, so these exorcism rituals and homemade remedies, though they were prepared calmly, methodically, were a sign of her desperation.

When the pain became so wrenching that she began to throw up this black, tarlike spatter, she couldn't deny what was happening anymore. She couldn't hide her desperation, or her humiliation at being so helpless, which was killing her as much as the cancer.

She tried each time to make it to the bathroom, but sometimes the coughing fits and the blackness that followed came on so suddenly that she didn't have time even to grab one of the towels she'd placed around the house. The first time I saw one of her fits, we were in the living room. The stuff shot out of her and landed on the couch and on the rug. I picked up a towel and rushed to hand it to her, to clean up, but she waved me away. She motioned for Papa, who had seen it before, to help. I think she wanted me to leave the room, but I stayed and I watched and I knew she wouldn't wave me away the next time. The next time I would have already heard the rattling cough and seen the black mess, and I would have remembered the humiliation in her eyes that made her look aged and pathetically childlike at the same time. And she would sit and allow both Papa and me to help.

Around Christmas she became worse, and I'd stop by the house nearly every day after work. Her appetite was nearly gone and she had difficulty walking, but she insisted on cooking. If Jimmy came by she'd rattle off a recipe for her biscotti or her panettone, which he'd write down in his fancy three-ring notebook with shiny pages. It was a project they were working on, this sort of formal handing down of the recipes that would sustain the rest of us. I don't know if I've ever seen them so happy together. Mama never relied on a standard set of ingredients, throwing in a handful of salt here, a scoop of butter there, but their project forced her to take stock of every grain, clove, and drop of food that slipped through her fingers. This was one of the reasons that she still wanted to cook. So she could pay attention, as if she were doing it for the first time, taking in the aroma of the anise, gauging its potency in terms of spoonfuls rather than the intuitive pinch or sprinkle. And it gave her something to think about, too. Plenty to think about.

A few weeks later she couldn't get out of bed. When she spoke, her mouth worked slowly, as if she were contemplating every word. Her eyes moved like dark glaciers as they panned the room, taking in every shadow, every corner. She hadn't eaten anything for days, so she'd dab at her dry lips with a wet rag, or we'd do it for her if she seemed too drowsy.

She spoke only Italian now. None of the hurried mincing of it with her broken English. And although her speech became slurred at times, from the morphine, I understood her perfectly. She didn't intend to eat again, which Papa and I respected, but which infuriated Jimmy, who claimed she was delirious, saying, "How can you starve her, goddamn it?" and pleaded for an IV at least. Since she was dying and knew she was dying, I expected certain profound words to spill out of her. Although this didn't happen, the things she said were stirring. "Can someone brush my hair?" she asked. She *asked*. "I'd like to hug," she said, trying to kid. "I'm ready to hug." We tried to choke back tears, to be strong for her, but she didn't need that. She lay there calmly, confident as usual, breathing through her mouth, doing what she had to do, like dying was another meal she had to put on the table and she was going to show us how it was done.

She died on a Thursday at three in the morning. The Wednesday before, friends filed through the house with armfuls of pasta and bread and pastries. A few broke down, but most of them, older Italian and Polish women in the neighborhood who had dressed in black nearly their entire lives, talked with Mama like they usually did, promising to pray for her, assuring her that her family would be taken care of. Mama responded when she could, but the nurse we'd hired kept her so drugged by then she could barely keep her eyes open.

I felt an ache in my throat as the last of the friends left. The screen door wheezed shut and clicked, and there was a finality in the click that made me shudder. It seemed that if the friends could stay, that nothing would happen to Mama. But it was also comforting to know that, since Papa and I decided that we wouldn't call an ambulance, she would die in a matter of hours, in her home, in her bed, with her family.

We sat around her—Papa and Jimmy and I—mostly in silence. We held her hands, brushed her forehead with our fingers. Her mouth was agape; her eyes rolled back into their sockets. From her throat came this muffled rattling, *rantolo,* a gray, ugly sound I never want to hear again.

"Mama," Jimmy whispered. "We're here for you, Mama."

"We're praying for you, Mama," I said.

She gave no sign that she'd heard us.

"Lucia," Papa said. *"Va bene. Puoi lasciare."* You can go now, he said.

With what must have been everything she had, she looked at her husband a last time. Only her eyes moved, her head immobile on the pillow. I'm not sure if she recognized him, but I'm fairly certain, though Jimmy will dispute this, that the corners of her mouth nudged, as if in a grin.

And then she let go, something she was never able to do as a mother or a wife. I think she really believed, as she liked to say, that if you eat, you never die, as if she would have the upper hand even with death. And in a way, maybe she did. Maybe she was right.

Sundays

GIACOMO

WHEN I THINK ABOUT MAMA IT IS ALWAYS SUNDAY.

I am ten and I saunter into the kitchen, waiting for Mama to turn away from the stove so I can pull a slice of warm bread from the newly baked loaf and dip it into the red sauce that percolates like hot molasses. It's a game we play, Mama lingering at the stove for minutes at a time, stirring, smiling, wondering probably about the depth of my patience. But I wait her out, return her sidelong glances with a placid grin meant to tease her. Or I point out the size of the plum tomatoes in the backyard, insisting she should take a look. Inevitably she turns and I move swiftly from loaf to pot to door, and I am gone, I think.

"Giacomo," she says. "Why you no sit?"

I freeze at the door. Steam rises from the bread and curls in front of my eyes.

"I'm going outside for a little while, Mama," I say to the door.

The morning sun is a flat patch of white.

"No, no, stay," she says and starts to follow, but I slip off without looking back, offering apologies over my shoulder, keeping the bread cupped to my chest. She'll get no farther than the doorway, I know, but I turn into our gangway anyway, out of Mama's view, my mouth already watering.

I am sixteen, gazing at the mound of homemade cavatelli and meatballs on Mama's table, wondering how I'm going to resist. She hasn't yet discovered that I must keep my weight down for this new sport of wrestling that she can't even begin to pronounce, and when she tries, she looks as if an unbearable bitterness is torturing her tongue. As far as I can recall, I did not join wrestling to spite Mama, but I cannot think of anything now that would agitate her more.

"Eat, Giacomo," she orders. "Eat more."

I stare at the clock. Just past noon. As if our hungers on Sundays can't wait. Do I tell her? Do I reveal that my postage-stamp world has been torn apart, that Sunday pasta is no longer the center of my existence? Do I tell her about the battles that I know lie ahead, or show that I can be as rock stubborn as she is?

Mama ladles her red sauce over each of our plates like she has done countless times before, unaware that this is a pivotal moment in our lives. But no one notices. Papa and Michael are hunched over their cavatelli, maybe thinking already about seconds.

I am twenty-two, waiting for Ray, who will join Mama and Papa and me for dinner at two o'clock and then take me back to our apartment. My tibia and fibula are not healed yet, but I can hobble around fairly well now after six weeks of lying around at home. Mama skitters around the kitchen, her movements more abrupt than usual as she tries to stifle the anger that smolders inside her. I regret dragging Ray into the middle of my leaving, but I know that Mama will be unbearable otherwise. I know that bringing in an outsider has been the only tactic to ever work with Mama, though I'm ashamed to use it at this point in my life.

Afternoon shadows darken half the living room where I have camped out for the past month and a half, and I watch Mama bounce back and forth between the light and dark.

"C'mon, Mama. You knew this was only temporary," I tell her.

"Temp?"

"You knew I wasn't going to stay."

"No stay. Go. No difference."

I snicker, trying to lighten her up, but she doesn't relent.

"I'm old lady," she says. "Pretty soon I go eh you no have to worry. No worry no more. *Caro Dio*."

She's close to tears, but I know she will hold back.

I lean forward, retrieve my crutches, and follow her as best I can from room to room.

"You crazy?" she says. "You fall. No go fast."

"I'm just trying to follow you, Mama," I say, out of breath. "I'll stop when you stop."

"*Stupido*."

"*Stupido*, yes."

"*Imbecille*."

"Yeah, I know."

In the kitchen she pauses finally but keeps her hands busy tossing the salad.

"I'm not moving to another country, Mama. Or to another state. Not even another city. I'm ten minutes away. Ten minutes. And"—I pause because I want this understood—"I'm not leaving because of you. I just need to be on my own. I'm not a boy anymore."

She looks up and examines me, as if this is a revelation, something she has never considered before. And then I see it. Unfolding like an envelope tamped down for years and now opened, the brown glue disintegrating like chalk dust. The corners of her mouth curl up as she transfers her pity from herself to me. "One day," she says. "One day you see."

The pity is misplaced, I know, wasted perhaps, but I am grateful nonetheless, and relieved finally.

Before I know it I'm pushing thirty-five and have to prepare now for the ritual Sunday evening dinner at Mama's. I fast the entire day, maybe even the day before—or at the very least eat light meals. A few hours before leaving I run through my calisthenics—though I haven't heard anyone call it that since high school—jumping jacks, squats, chin-ups, push-ups—and sit-ups, the way I used to do them in P.E., bending all the way up with my hands cradling the back of my head, my elbows grazing my knees before easing down again.

I wouldn't have thought it possible, but the sheer quantity of food that appears on Mama's table has increased with each passing year, a natural consequence of grandchildren, but the increase is in no way proportional to that. My brother, Michael, were he to notice, would likely glare at my gut and blame me for the extra food, food that we later haul off in boxes to our cars during drawn-out good-byes, Mama on our heels with a bag of biscotti or *taralli* or some other treat we insist we don't need but know better than to argue about. Loading the cars takes us three or four trips.

Pulling away from the curb saddens me. Because I know that Mama is preoccupied with that one last bag she could have filled for us. She glances back at the house, as if thinking, *What else can I give them? I haven't given them enough.* I don't know how to tell her that she has always given all that she could.

Dusk begins to settle around the car, Teri buckled in next to me, the girls strapped in the backseat, waving to Grandma and Grandpa one last time. In the rearview mirror, Papa disappears toward the house, and Mama is left with her hand in the air, as if in benediction, a street statue washed in fiery sienna from the last splinters of sunlight. As I watch her recede into the branches of the maples and oak trees that line her block, I know that I will someday miss this moment, that I will look back and wonder where I was rushing off to while Mama stood there rooted, finally rooted, holding onto the modest hope that next Sunday would bring us all together again.

ALSO BY TONY ROMANO

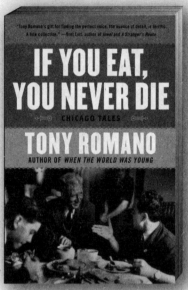

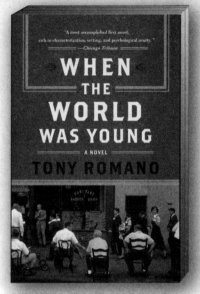

IF YOU EAT, YOU NEVER DIE
Chicago Tales

ISBN 978-0-06-085794-3 (paperback)

In a masterful evocation of time and place, Tony Romano introduces readers to the Comingos, a first generation Italian-American family. The evocative stories in this collection shed light on the inner secrets and desires of these Italian immigrants, the restlessness and self-searching of the sons, Michelino (Michael) and Giacomo (Jimmy), and the ever-distant American childhood of the four young granddaughters, weaving together two dozen stories into a stunning, cohesive family history.

"Suffused with a quiet grace and a sweet passion."
—David Michael Kaplan, author of *Comfort* and *Skating in the Dark*

WHEN THE WORLD WAS YOUNG
A Novel

ISBN 978-0-06-085793-6 (paperback)

It's the summer of 1957. In the heart of Chicago, first-generation Italian immigrants Angela Rosa and Agostino Peccatori are caught between worlds. Far from home and with five children born in the United States, the Peccatori family is left clinging to old country ways in an era of upending change. While Agostino spends his days running the neighborhood trattoria, Mio Fratello, Angela Rosa must face the building tension at home as her children struggle to define themselves within a family rooted in tradition.

"Tony Romano can indeed write . . . a multilayered, often dark and edgy saga." —*Philadelphia Inquirer*